W9-BPM-750

A HEALTHY PLACE
TO DIE

Also by Peter King

Death Al Dente
Dying on the Vine
Spiced to Death
The Gourmet Detective

Peter King

A HEALTHY PLACE TO DIE
A Gourmet Detective Mystery

St. Martin's Minotaur ✎ New York

www.stmartins.com

Library of Congress Cataloging-in-Publication Data

King, Peter (Christopher Peter), date.
    A healthy place to die : a Gourmet Detective mystery / Peter King.—1st ed.
        p.   cm.
    ISBN 0-312-24269-7
    1. Gourmet Detective (Fictitious character)—Fiction. 2. Resorts—
Switzerland—Fiction. 3. Switzerland—Fiction. 4. Gourmets—Fiction.
5. Cookery—Fiction. I. Title.

PS3561.I4822 H43 2000
813'.54—dc21
                                                                99-089783

First Edition: July 2000

10   9   8   7   6   5   4   3   2   1

A HEALTHY PLACE
TO DIE

CHAPTER ONE

C ome along now, Mr. Armitage—we haven't drunk our spa water yet—swallow it right down."

I had three objections to this proposal.

One—I didn't intend to drink spa water without tasting it.

Two—I don't really like water.

Three—and most important of all—my name is not Armitage.

This was not the best time to debate these points though. Instead I said, "Nurse, if *we* are going to drink spa water, you take yours first. Leave some for me."

She smiled, a wide beautiful smile that made full use of her generous red lips, glistening white teeth, and slightly smoky blue eyes. "Now, Mr. Armitage—remember your briefing when you checked in this morning. My name is Julia and that's what you should call me. See—here it is, right here."

She used one long, exquisitely manicured forefinger to tap the smart plastic badge with its thin metal trim. My eyes involuntarily followed her motion, and it was hard to tear them away for the badge was attached to that part of her trim uniform that molded one of her two most prominent features. I looked at the badge—it confirmed that she was "Julia" just as she had said, but I kept on looking anyway.

The word *nurse* that she disapproved of was nontheless appropriate according to that morning's briefing on my arrival here at the Alpine Springs Spa and Health Resort in Switzerland. All of the staff were qualified nurses, but they avoided use of the term as they emphasized that this was not a hospital or a sanitarium.

The female members of the staff were certainly carefully chosen. I had seen only half a dozen of them so far, but all were blond, buxom, and beautiful. None of them was more than an inch below six feet and a further distinction from the "nurse" classification was the uniform. The fit was more suited to a Fifth Avenue fashion show runway, and the color was a soft, warm cream that had anything but clinical connotations.

She smiled again and I could not resist. "All right, Julia. Leave the water. I'll drink it in a minute."

"Good. I'll be back in a little while. Here's our handbook—you might want to look through it, get familiar with us." I doubted that a double entendre was hidden there, but she added, "An analysis of our spa water is on page thirty-seven." I watched her walk away until she was out of sight and wished she had walked slower so I could enjoy the view longer.

I was sitting in a wrought-iron chair with a comfortably padded seat and backrest at a wrought-iron table with a thick glass top. The lawn I was on was not quite big enough to accommodate the landing of the space shuttle, but it was flat and smooth as a billiard table and intensely green. The main spa building looked as if it had been transported from Tuscany, and behind it, sweeping toward the foothills of the Alps, tier after tier of grapevines were in geometrically perfect rows.

Housing was in minichalets around the main building. They were sumptuously furnished and decorated in light pastel colors. Shuttered French doors at the back led to a private terrace. The emperor-size beds had fluffy pillows and the bathrooms were large for Europe, with sunken tubs that had more controls than a jet fighter. The refrigerators were stocked with champagnes, wines, Swiss cheeses, and snacks, and a fireplace was laid with logs. The rooms were not only air-conditioned but offered a dialed choice of room fragrances.

I looked across the lawn to where a small group was doing tai chi exercises. All were dressed in loose-fitting track suits, each one a different color—sky blue, lemon yellow, carmine red, bright purple. . . . Arms outstretched, feet wide apart, they looked from here like toys whose batteries were running down. Near to me, a man sat at a table reading. He was ruddy faced and heavily built with a magnificent shock of white hair.

In the other direction, leading into hundreds of acres of grassy slopes, were pathways and wide staircases leading to the hydrotherapy center. All were built from a wood with a color that gave them a distinctly Japanese look accentuated by curli-cues and carved trim. The tour that was part of the initial in-doctrination had been conducted by Norma, a clone of Julia but even more voluptuous if that was possible. She had explained that the hydrotherapy facilities included Roman baths, Turkish steam baths, Swiss high-pressure shower jets, Japanese soaking tubs, Hungarian mud baths, a tunnel that provided seaweed flag-ellation, herbal Jacuzzis, and even prosaic whirlpools, saunas, and just plain pools. To be fair, they were not really that plain . . . the sides and base of the pool were perfect mirrors.

It was a gorgeous day with a few streaky cirrus clouds trying desperately to break the monotony of the light blue sky and not being very successful. It was warm, in late summer, and Norma had reminded us of the unequaled purity of the air here in the Swiss Alps. She had taken us through the environ-mental center where banks of instruments and dials and digital panels gave a vast amount of information, including a continual analysis of the air.

On the table, the cut-glass tumbler of water sat waiting to be drunk. I could not disappoint Julia even though that might make her pout in that delightful way she had. I drank a sip of water, leaned back, and gave it my own taste analysis. It wasn't that bad, not too salty, and the mineral content was on the verge of effervescence.

Forgetting about page thirty-seven, I drank the whole glassful.

The tai chi group concluded its session, and a few minutes later four women came out in brief outfits and started tossing a clear plastic ball the size of a VW Beetle. I could not understand their purpose—if there was one—but it did not matter as the players were more watchable than the game.

"Perhaps you'd like to join them the next time they play."

I had not heard Julia's approach—the lush lawn muffled her footsteps.

"I'll have more energy then from all these minerals," I told her, aware that she had looked at my empty glass.

"I've brought you the luncheon menu." She handed me a tall card in pastel colors. "I thought you might want a little time to study it. Can I bring you a cocktail first?"

"You know, Julia, this is an extraordinary place."

Her big smoky blue eyes widened, and she treated me to a miniversion of that delicious pout. "Extraordinary? In what way?"

"Well, it's true I haven't been to a spa before, but I had a completely different impression of what they're like. I wouldn't have thought that cocktails were a part of the diet."

She looked hurt. She pressed one hand against her heart. It had the effect of squeezing the already tight fabric of her uniform up around her breast.

"Diet! My goodness, that's a word we never use here. In fact, you'll find that there are a lot of words and expressions that we never use. As you will recall from our brochure, our entire approach is to provide a lifestyle that is opulent in every way. You can eat and drink as much as you want—and anything you want, exercise only a little—in fact, you come here to enjoy yourself in every way."

It sounded great, and I told her so.

She took her hand away and gently smoothed her uniform back into place. The effect was as erotic as a stripper on Bourbon Street. "But this is why you came here, I'm sure," she said. "Our brochure stresses that this is our central theme. You can enjoy a luxurious holiday with every amenity you could wish and at the same time, you can lose weight, recuperate from an illness or an addiction, be treated for a physical or mental affliction."

"I can have my cake and eat it." I did not want to admit that I hadn't read the brochure and didn't know all this.

"You can enjoy the bliss of eating a cake but have none of the drawbacks associated with having eaten it."

"How do you do all that?"

She looked coy—or at least as coy as a six-foot buxom blonde built like a brick outbuilding can look. She did an awfully good job of it too.

"Come now, Mr. Armitage, you wouldn't want me to reveal any of our secrets, would you?"

"And I'll bet you have a lot of them."

She shook her head and the blond hair danced.

"You'd be surprised how much of it is common sense and careful planning. Miss de Witt is very good at both of those."

I had met Caroline de Witt, the executive director, on my arrival. Raven-black hair (did she select blondes for staff as deliberate contrast? I wondered), statuesque, cool as ice, and capable of charming a hungry cobra. "I'm sure she's good at a lot of things."

"She is." Julia was sincere. "She's exceptionally good at everything. Did you decide on a cocktail?"

"As this is my first day, I think I will. Make it a whiskey sour. With rye."

"Very well. Did you make your luncheon choices?"

"Not yet. I'll make a decision by the time you get back with the drink. By the way, my name is not Armitage." Her wide blue eyes opened wider as I explained.

When I finished, she nodded and walked away with that swinging long-legged stride that strained the seams of her tight uniform.

Another clone of Julia was talking to the ruddy-faced man at the nearby table. They were having a discussion about the menu, but I could not hear what they were saying. The blonde was nodding and picking up the menu. The man had evidently made his choice for luncheon. She walked off with the same stride as Julia—well, no, not exactly; this was a little looser but just as visual. I got up, taking the menu with me, and walked across the impossibly green carpet of grass. It was time to do something.

After all, I wasn't here for my health.

CHAPTER TWO

So why was I here?

It was a fair question, and I mentally debated if the answer was also fair. It seemed straightforward enough. I had been sitting in my small office in Hammersmith in West London, answering mail. The first letter was from a soft-drink producer that wanted to know if I would be one of the judges in a lemonade-tasting contest. I set that aside under a paperweight that was the base of a one-hundred-year-old champagne bottle. That was my "decline" stack, and I thought it very appropriate.

The second letter was more interesting. It was from a man who had contacted me on a couple of previous occasions. He was a technical specialist at the Elmwood Film Studios and had asked me for advice on ancient foods and cooking equipment. This time, he was working on a film set in the seventeenth century, and he had a banquet scene to shoot. He was looking for any help I could give him to make this authentic. He had access to studio experts, but he liked to check with me too, he said.

I jotted down a few notes. First, he should make sure that no forks appeared on the table, as these had still not become common usage in 1600. Most people still ate with their fingers, although knives would be on the table. These would be the dagger type of all-purpose knife that could be used for both cutting and eating. Spoons were common, and several sizes would be evident.

Large roasts of beef and pork would be on platters—of silver if it was a really rich household, or wood otherwise. On the table would also be large whole salmon, geese, capons, crabs, lobsters, oysters, mussels, eels, and smoked herring. When the host wished to impress, his guests would be offered carp, three to four feet long, lampreys, turtles, and giant frogs. If the film-makers wanted to risk some of the food becoming talking points for the audience, they could add peacocks and swans to the spread.

Bowls of soup and grain puddings full of meat strips would be seen, as well as plates of pastries, pies, and fritters; bowls of sauce; and loaves of bread of different kinds and shapes—but, of course, none with the shape of a mass-produced loaf, as that is merely a modern packing convenience. Guests would be drinking wine, mead, and beer.

It was the practice until the nineteenth century for all of these dishes to be on the table at the same time, so this feast would be authentic as well as photogenic.

As to why a technician at a movie studio should be asking me a question like this, well, I operate my business under the name of "The Gourmet Detective." I'm not a detective at all, you understand. I seek out rare spices and food ingredients that are hard to locate. I advise on cooking methods and foods from past eras. I recommend substitutes for rare and expensive ingredients. On a few occasions, such investigations have led me into some dangerous situations and even violence—something I eschew.

I was concluding with a draft of a letter accepting an invitation to be on a wine-tasting panel (a responsibility I never shirk) when the phone rang.

It was Carver Armitage, an acquaintance for some years. Carver is a journalist who, after spending some years in the city reporting on financial matters, had decided that food was a fast-growing subject of reader interest and a more lucrative subject than bearer bonds. This had coincided with Carver's becoming intrigued with cooking. Instead of picking up frozen dinners at Safeway, he was now actually buying the components of a meal and cooking them.

He called me a couple of times that period, both times to ask why a foolproof dish had gone wrong, refusing to accept the obvious answer. I had partly lost touch with him after that, although I often saw his name in newspapers and magazines as his star rose in the world of cuisine. He appeared on TV, talking about food, introducing famous chefs, and even cooking meals and explaining them step by step.

He was calling now from St. Giles's Hospital, he told me. "Not something you ate, I hope," I said, a little unkindly. He chuckled. It was hollow but still a chuckle.

"I'm only in for some tests and observation," he explained.

"Anything serious?" I asked, wanting to make up for my opening gaffe.

"No, just one those male things," he said airily, and I recalled that St. Giles's was said to have the best male-impotence clinic in the country. All of the witty retorts that suggested themselves were resolutely thrust from my mind, and I merely said, "Anything I can do?"

"As a matter of fact, there is. It's the reason for my call. See, there's an event coming up next week in Switzerland. It's at a spa. Lectures, talks, cooking classes, you know the kind of thing. Well, I'm booked as one of the speakers and demonstrators.

I thought this visit here to St. Giles was going to be a couple of days or so. Now they tell me I have to stay here another week. So I need a substitute."

"Try Jim Dillard," I said. "Right up his street."

"I did. He's in Australia. Won't be back in time."

"What about Jean-Marc Separdel, the chef at Antonio's? A real comer, folks love that accent. He's inventive. . . ."

"He's in Bangkok, opening a branch restaurant there."

"Louis Ibenido—he has a few offbeat ideas, I know, but he's a great talker and can whip up a soufflé faster than you can say Paul Bocuse."

"He can't do it—he's knee-deep in preparing a TV series, and they're behind schedule."

I produced a few other names, but Carver said he had already tried them without success. I was pondering other possibilities when he said, "I don't suppose you'd be interested in doing it?"

I truly had not even considered it. His call had been a surprise and so had his inquiry, which I had taken literally to mean that he wanted me to recommend someone.

"Me?" I said.

"Sure. You've done this stuff before."

"Only a few times . . ."

"You're an expert."

"I wouldn't say that."

"You're familiar with various cooking styles."

"Some," I admitted modestly, and from then on I was increasingly committed. Finally, I said yes upon his adding, "You can, of course, have the whole of my fee."

———

Julia listened to a highly condensed version of this good reason why I did not call myself Armitage. She smiled pleasantly. "Well, you are very welcome here, even if you are a substitute." I hadn't listed for her the names of all those earlier choices, who, for one reason or another, had been unable to be present. I looked at Julia; I looked around at the impossibly white peaks of the Alps, and I reflected that being a substitute was not too bad, after all.

I gave her my order for lunch—pear endive, and blue cheese salad with lemon-thyme vinaigrette followed by pan-seared wild salmon with a Burgundy-citrus coulis. "We recommend these without any accompaniments," said Julia sweetly. "As we do most lunch dishes. You are, of course, quite free to—"

"No, no," I concurred, trying to avoid sounding too goody-goody. "That's fine."

CHAPTER THREE

Before luncheon on my first day here, I had introduced myself to the white-haired man at the nearby table. He was Tim Reynolds, and as soon as he told me his name, I recognized him as one of the golf greats of the past.

"Come here every year," he told me. "Fine place. None of that diet nonsense. Wonderful food, perfect service. Your first time?"

He had put on weight since his glory days, and his face was showing a slight puffiness that suggested not only good food and drink but plenty of it. He was affable and friendly, though, and he showed interest when I explained how I came to be there.

"Carver Armitage? Oh, yes, seen his column. So you're replacing him? Demonstrations start tomorrow, I believe."

"Yes. Are you going to be there? Wouldn't have had you pegged as wanting to learn how to cook."

"Coincidence more than anything. I come here once a year, and this year it just happens to be at the same time as this cooking festival. Don't do much cooking myself, but I need a new interest and thought this might be it, so I signed up." He gave me a wink. "Got a job on your hands, trying to teach me to cook."

"Anybody can learn," I assured him. "Still play any golf?"

"There's a nine-hole course over there." He waved past the main building. "Not too hard, but it keeps me loosened up." He gave me an appraising look, as if trying to decide whether to confide in me. In a lowered tone, he said with a conspiratorial air, "There's just one thing I don't like about this place."

"Really? What's that?"

"It deprives me of the satisfaction of being able to smuggle booze in." He broke into a laugh, and I joined him.

"Had a lot of experience at that, have you?"

"You'd better believe it. I guess I'm something of a spa buff. I really like these places, been to lots of them all over the world. Trouble with so many of them is that they behave like missionaries—want to reform your body, help you lose weight, tinker with your health. The way they all start is by saying 'no alcohol.' "

He lowered his voice again, this time to a confidential level. "Not that I'm a drunk. Oh, I've been close to it many a time— even when I was on the circuit. But I like to come to a place like this to enjoy myself, not be preached at and monitored. Certainly not to be a teetotaler."

"I don't have that much experience of spas," I said, "but I find this place unusual in that regard too. No alcohol is the first rule in many of them, I understand, and as for smokers, most places would refer them to Devil's Island rather than accept them."

"They're smart—Caroline de Witt and Leighton Vance. They know that people like to be pampered. That's what they do here. Best spa I know."

I had left him after lunch to take part in a briefing session. About a dozen of us were there in a state-of-the-art conference room, where Caroline de Witt, the striking dark-haired director of the spa, introduced everyone.

Marta Giannini was a face I knew at once, for she had been a longtime movie heartthrob of mine. I gallantly refused to calculate how old she was, for she had not been on the screen in some time. She told us in her delightful accent and quite without rancor that for purely financial reasons, she was going to undertake a series of television commercials featuring a major food product. The producers had asked her to attend the classes here at the spa in order to develop a familiarity with kitchens and their equipment.

"How could I refuse?" she asked with a lovely smile. "The food here is so good. The atmosphere is wonderfully relaxing. Besides, I know nothing about cooking."

Gunther Probst, a reserved, quiet Austrian, was a computer genius, it seemed. He had plans for putting recipes on software and wanted to get some firsthand immersion in food and cooking. Millicent Manners was a fluffy blonde who appeared convinced that every eye was on her. (It was true that many were.) She was going to star in a TV soap opera series set in a restaurant and said she "wanted to soak up the atmosphere."

The presenters, demonstrators, and speakers were introduced in turn. Michel Leblanc was short and roly-poly, a TV chef of renown in France. Bradley Thompson was a fast-food millionaire from Canada and intended to shed a new and more favorable light on fast foods, he said. Kathleen Evans was a slim, fair-haired young woman who wrote a food column syndicated in several countries. Helmut Helberg from Stuttgart was the owner of a supermarket chain. He was big and jolly and said his mission was to improve the bond between the sellers of good food and its consumers.

Axel Vorstahl had a well-known restaurant in Copenhagen and had been responsible for many of the kitchens on Scandinavian cruise ships. Oriana Frascati was a New Yorker but with all the looks and characteristics of an Italian background. She was editor of Kitchen Press, a prominent publisher of cookbooks. I completed the lineup and had to endure being addressed as "Armitage" a few more times.

Caroline de Witt then introduced Leighton Vance. He was to lead the demonstrations of cooking techniques. He should be on TV, I thought. He was in his early forties, with movie-star good looks and a genial personality. His wife, Mallory, was one of the sous-chefs. Demure and pretty, a few years younger than her husband, she seemed to be very much in his shadow.

The audience was largely amateur as far as practical cooking was concerned. A few worked in the trade in other capacities and others had tangential interest in food, for instance Marta Giannini, Millicent Manners, and Gunther Probst. Schedules were presented, timetables agreed upon and some guidelines indicated. Caroline asked each presenter to describe in brief detail the substance of their presentation in order to avoid duplication.

As we broke up, I sought out Marta Giannini. Her luminous, wide-set eyes brightened as I told her how much I had enjoyed her films. She still looked good up close with her high cheekbones and generous mouth, and her figure was still eye-catching despite a few added pounds. "I enjoy my films too," she told me with an intimate smile. "I watch them any time they are on television. I saw *Stolen Love* last night."

"The ending's too sad for me," I said. "You think Victor is dead and you go into a convent. He comes looking for you, can't find you, and thinks *you* are dead. He goes on one last dangerous mission and is killed. His body is brought to your convent."

"It was sad," she agreed. "But we had so much fun making it!"

"I was astounded when you said you knew nothing about cooking. You wrote a cookbook some years ago."

"Pooh! That was written for me. They just paid me to use my name on the cover and put photographs of me all through the book."

"Photographs in kitchens," I reminded her.

She shook her head, still smiling. "No, they were studio photographs. They superimposed them on photos of kitchens."

We chatted further. Her memory was extraordinary when it came to her films. She remembered every person with whom she had ever worked, every twist of every plot, and had a fund of stories about happenings on the set.

I tore myself away reluctantly. I could have basked in the light of those gorgeous eyes all morning, but I wanted to talk to as many people as possible. Helmut Helberg was looking round the room with something of the same purpose in mind, so we coincided.

He was almost the stereotypical German—but his voice was not the deep booming projection that I expected. He spoke in a normal tone and his English was excellent. "Ah, Mr. Armitage," he greeted me. "I have been wanting to meet you for a long time."

After I had straightened him out on that misapprehension, he told me of his desire to improve the supermarket system. "We have let it get out of control," he was saying, and his sincerity made up for his lack of volume. "The supermarket has become too impersonal, too cold."

"The very factors that cause people to long for the days of

the small corner shop where the owner knew all his customers and they got personalized service."

"Exactly. What we must do is combine the size and efficiency of today's supermarket with those characteristics."

"A difficult task," I commiserated.

"That is what I am going to be talking about. How difficult it is and what we must do to achieve it."

"I'll be listening," I promised.

Kathleen Evans was a slim young career woman. I had read her column on occasion and knew her to be provocative and caustic. At first I thought she belied that persona, but a few minutes' conversation with her convinced me that she was just as tough as her column. Her fair hair stopped just short of being blond and her eyes, though blue, were unrelenting. Perhaps that was because her initial reaction to me was one of deep suspicion.

"Who are you? You're not Carver Armitage!"

"It's true," I admitted. "I am not now, nor have I ever been, Carver Armitage." I explained who I was and why I was there. She was not mollified. "Where is Carver?"

"He's in St. Giles's Hospital in London."

"What's he doing there?"

"Having treatment for a minor ailment."

Her hostility did not abate. "He was perfectly well the last time I saw him."

"Yes, well, his ailment did not prevent him from carrying out normal duties."

Her eyes glinted like blue rock. "So he sent you to replace him." Her voice indicated what an impossible task she thought that to be.

"As best I can," I said lightly.

She studied me for a moment and I prepared further a defense, but it was not needed. She switched subjects. "Leighton Vance is one of the most underrated chefs I know," she declared. "Maybe this conference will help to raise him up where he belongs."

"It's an excellent opportunity," I agreed.

She was evidently a fervent supporter of Vance and his cooking. She praised him highly, said she had publicized him in her column and thought him bold and imaginative.

"Increasingly rare talents in a chef," I agreed. Such enthusiasm in his favor seemed at odds with her generally critical attitude.

"He and Caroline run a great operation here. Everything about it is first class."

"You sound as if you've been here before."

"Once or twice," she said offhandedly.

I wanted to talk to Axel Vorstahl. I had spent a part of my early career as a chef on cruise ships and was anxious to learn what had changed since then with the still-continuing boom in cruise travel. He was in a deep conversation, but I saw Michel Leblanc, the French chef. He was talking to Gunther Probst, the computer whiz, and as both gave me an inviting smile I joined them.

Inevitably, the topic moved to French cuisine. As tactfully as I could, I asked if perhaps the eminent position of French cuisine was threatened.

"Very much so," Leblanc admitted. "I strongly believe that interest in the Oriental cuisines in recent years is responsible."

Probst was surprised. "Oriental cuisines?"

"Yes. They offer meals with lowered fat and reduced cholesterol. They are simple to prepare and fast to cook. All our top chefs in France recognized these advantages and began to incorporate their characteristics into our cuisine."

"Isn't it true that these changes initiated the nouvelle cuisine?" I asked.

"Certainly. Alain Senderens, Gerard Besson, Fredy Girardet all acknowledged this."

"But how did this threaten the dominant position of French cooking?" Probst wanted to know.

"The novelty wore off too quickly," said Leblanc. "Also, it was perhaps too abrupt a change to make in so short a time. The French—and many other nations cooking in the French style—were used to their sauces and richer methods of food preparation."

"Is this the secret of the spa?" I asked. "Do we see here the realization that while really rich foods—high cholesterols and high saturated fat, salt and sodium—must be modified, neither do we want to go too lean and mean? Is a compromise better achieved here than in most places?"

"Sounds reasonable to me," said Probst, "but then I'm still learning some of the terminology. It's as specialized as computerspeak."

Leblanc nodded. "It is one of the reasons I was delighted to get the invitation to come to this conference again. I wanted to see for myself just why the spa is so successful. There is no question that the food is a major factor."

The discussion went on, Probst being concerned with leaping in periodically to query a word or an expression and Leblanc showing a good understanding of the responsibilities—and problems—of a good chef. He would be a chef-owner in a very short time, that was my analysis.

During this conversation, we had drifted in the direction

of the long table that covered the wall nearest the double doors. It contained various kinds of coffee and tea as well as snacks and soft drinks. We had reached a crisis, Leblanc and I. We did not see eye-to-eye on the leveling effect—if any—of the European Community on the individuality of the cuisines of the various nations composing it. Leblanc was wagging an admonishing finger at me as he prepared to make a vital point.

It was then that the double doors flung open and a newcomer entered the room.

CHAPTER FOUR

She was one of those women who display presence and personality without being domineering or sexist. She was also a woman who was clearly attractive, and yet it was not easy to identify any of the notable characteristics of beauty. She had a strong face with slightly high cheekbones, large brown eyes, and light brown hair that fell straight as if it were natural. She was fairly tall and almost athletic in build.

"I believe I'm late," she announced without a hint of apology. "Can't blame Swissair. I missed my flight."

The room hadn't exactly fallen silent when she walked in, but most of its occupants were aware of her entrance. Then conversations resumed as Caroline de Witt went to her and they exchanged words. "Let me introduce you around," Caroline said as she approached the nearest group, which happened to be our trio.

"This is Elaine Dunbar," she said, presenting the newcomer. When Caroline had told her who we were, I said to her, "You missed the part where we all tell what we do and why we are here."

She gave me a cool look and asked in a firm voice with no identifiable origin, "And just what do you all do and why are you here?"

It wasn't what I had in mind, but it was another means to the same end. We all told her and waited for her contribution.

"I'm a lawyer. I just got my J.D. My fiancé bought me the package to spend the week here as a reward."

"An unusual compensation," said Probst drily.

"Not at all. I intend to specialize in law as it pertains to food and restaurants. What more natural way to prepare for that kind of career?"

"It's still unusual," I commented. "The culinary business doesn't have many legal specialists—in fact, I can't think of any. Perhaps it needs a few. There must be lots of opportunities."

"But we are a very law-abiding vocation," Leblanc protested. "Do we need lawyers?"

"Not until you're in trouble," Elaine Dunbar said calmly. "Then you come screaming to us."

Leblanc looked ready to respond vigorously, his male Gallic blood aroused, but Probst defused him, saying lazily, "Have a lot of occasions to need lawyers in the computer business. Glad to have them on my side—it was always the ones on the other side I hated."

Caroline took the newcomer off to meet another group. I hoped none of them knew any lawyer jokes or that they would exercise restraint if they did. Elaine Dunbar looked as if she could be a tough customer in a debate.

There was not much more opportunity to talk to any of the other participants. All were anxious to get out into the extensive grounds and enjoy the glorious Alpine sunshine. The sun must have been hot down at lower altitudes, but we were about three thousand feet up the western slopes of the Schondig, whose peak tapered into the azure sky as if reaching to claw down an unwary cloud. Periodic breezes rolled up from the valley to keep the temperature at a perfect level.

I strolled across the grass and stood on the shore of the lake. On the far side, small craft were lined up awaiting customers. Kayaks, canoes, rowboats, and small sailcraft were there but nothing powered. Nobody was out today and a flock of birds was dining noisily, undisturbed. Down toward the valley, I caught sight of movement. Two horses were coming up the slope, and I recalled that stables were another attraction of the spa. It did not seem to lack any of the entertaining amenities, I thought. I was anxious too to see the mud baths, saunas, steam baths, and similar aids to health, but they would have to wait.

This was a good chance to take a look at the kitchens. Stainless steel was everywhere, gleaming, glistening, reflecting from bench tops, splash shields, burner racks. The wooden chopping blocks were spotless and looked alien against the groups of bright orange, indigo blue, and charcoal black ceramic stoves and hoods. These were trimmed with copper, and among them I noted the very newest features such as magnetic induction burners that cook without producing heat and infrared covers that maintain heat without drying. A most unusual sight in a professional kitchen was the large windows, framing a fairy-tale picture of snowcapped peaks in the distance.

As it was late in the afternoon, the kitchen was quiet. The hustle and bustle would soon be starting as preparations got under way for the evening meal, but right now only two young women were active. One of them was Mallory Vance, the pretty, shy wife of Leighton. She was preparing a terrine of duck, laying the sliced duck breast into strips of prosciutto and sprinkling it liberally with wild rice, dried apricots, pistachio nuts, dried cherries, and a blend of spices. Before folding the prosciutto over it, she drizzled a generous amount of brandy on the mixture.

"Beautifully done," I complimented her, and she looked up, startled. Then she recognized me and smiled delightfully.

"*Garde-manger* usually comes off a mechanized production line today," I said. "It's nice to see it made properly, that is to say, by hand."

"Not many people call it that anymore," she said, reaching for more slices of duck breast. "You know what it means? 'The preservation of what is eaten.' "

"Yes. I believe that in former days, it referred to ways of using up scraps of meat, poultry, game, and fish that had been left over in the kitchen. Then the term was applied to the piece of kitchenware that was designed to store those scraps—a smaller larder, built of wood and with a wire mesh front. An apprentice chef had the task of keeping it supplied with ice."

"You are well informed," she said in surprise.

"It's my job," I said, and explained that I was obliged to live up to my sobriquet of "the Gourmet Detective." The history of food and a knowledge of what foods were eaten and how they were prepared and cooked in earlier times and civilizations were a part of my work.

She was listening, but only partly. She had stopped moving her hands, and a thick slice of duck breast stood uncut. When I finished, she said with wide eyes, "You're a detective?"

I explained further, emphasizing the food aspects and skimming over the times when my investigations had led to danger and even death. "I see," she said, mollified. I supposed detectives were rare in a law-abiding country like Switzerland, and she was a quiet, reserved young woman. She probably spent most of her time in the kitchen and saw little of the outside world.

She was about to say something when a harsh voice from behind me said, "We don't allow people in the kitchen." It was Leighton Vance. He wore light pants and a dark blue blazer with white shoes. His crisp white shirt sported a light blue ascot, which, though dated, suited his dashing image. He looked like a country squire who had just come back from a stroll through the village, nodding to his serfs.

"That's all right," I said easily. "As this whole week revolves around kitchens and what they produce and how they do it, naturally I was curious to see this one."

"You'll be in the kitchen enough during the presentations," he said, and his voice was still steely. "Otherwise, our rule is no outsiders."

"I was congratulating your wife on her technique with the terrine. She's an expert in an area that doesn't receive much attention today."

His handsome face was set in a hard cast and even a quiff of golden hair seemed to be bristling. My attempt to stretch the conversation was failing. I could see that as he said, "We are all experts here. It's why we are so successful. We hope to see you at dinner."

I knew when I wasn't wanted. I gave Mallory an extra-big smile as I left, just to irritate him.

As I prepared for dinner, I was wondering about the strange attitude of Leighton Vance. A week of cooking classes was about to begin—and Vance wanted to throw me out of his kitchen! What could be there that he wanted to hide? Yet I recalled more than a few chefs I knew who were jealously protective of their trade secrets. Many of them did not allow strangers in their kitchens, though most were a little more diplomatic in the way they ushered them out when caught. When the classes commenced, the kitchens would be open to scrutiny by all of the class members. Any secrets would be difficult to hide. So if such secrets were not in the kitchen, where could they be?

In the food—was that the answer? It seemed unlikely. An operation as prestigious as this would be very unlikely to be doing anything clandestine along those lines, and, in addition, the Swiss authorities are very strict in all matters concerning tourism. I was still puzzling when I went to dinner.

The main restaurant was high ceilinged and lit by four giant chandeliers. Wood-paneled walls gave it a slight feeling of period, but all else was modern while still maintaining a sense of tradition. Tables were set for eight, and place settings were shown on a large display at the entrance. It was also noted that settings would be changed every lunch and dinner so that everyone could enjoy a variety of dinner companions.

Next to me, a large gray-haired man with a look of authority introduced himself. He was Karl Wengen, a member of Switzerland's Nationalrat, the national council of 196 men. "All men?" I asked, a little surprised.

"Women in Switzerland were first granted a vote in 1953," he told me. "We have very few in governmental posts." He waited for me to comment, but I didn't want to generate a debate on that subject—at least, not before eating. He represented the canton of Aargau, one of the largest in the country, and told me that he came here once a year. "I come for my health," he said, patting his considerable stomach. "Others go to diet spas, but I prefer to come here. I may not lose weight, but this is the only place that restores my peace of mind."

On the other side sat a school principal from Denmark who said she was fulfilling a life ambition now that she had retired from teaching. Oriana Frascati, the cookbook editor, was across the table, deep in conversation with a Swiss agronomist who, from the snatches of conversation I could pick up, was telling of his recent U.N. mission to Mongolia.

I had been curious about the food here. I knew it was not diet oriented but neither did I expect the quality of Taillevent in Paris or La Grenouille in New York. Still, everyone spoke so highly of it that it had to be exceptional. I resolutely stifled any thought that because Leighton Vance had thrown me out of his kitchen (well, almost), he could not be a great chef. Any such illogicality would be unworthy of me, I decided.

The choices on the menu were numerous without being overwhelming. It takes longer to read some menus than it takes to eat the meal, and one can justifiably question whether every ingredient is fresh. I selected the mussel and vegetable salad, a deliberately low-key dish, so as to establish whether the chef could elevate it. The member from the Aargau had a Waldorf salad with smoked venison and black currant dressing, whereas the school principal preferred the creme Antillaise, a Caribbean soup based on spinach, rice, and coconut cream. Only one at our table asked for the confit of duck that Mallory had worked so hard to prepare.

My salad was warm, which was an encouraging start. It takes a clever chef to know which ingredients of a salad are fuller flavored when warmed. Shallots and chervil spiked the flavor even further, whereas a lesser chef would have used capers or anchovies, both too strong in a warm salad. Full marks to the chef, I thought, and reflected that it was a shame he could not know how fair I was being. My companions praised their dishes, and compliments could be heard from adjoining tables.

A tiny bowl of consommé served as an entremet, a

between-courses palate cleanser, much more sensible than the fruit sorbet that some restaurants serve. For the fish course, several of us went for the *omble chevalier*, the small salmon trout that is unique to Lac Leman, the lake around Geneva. Others had red snapper from the Mediterranean or Röteln, a trout caught around Zug, almost in the center of Switzerland. The *omble chevalier* came in a sorrel sauce that did not overcome the delicate taste of the fish. On the table were two bottles of white wine to accompany this course. One was a French Moselle and the other a Sauvignon from the Cielo vineyard in Italy.

The pattern of the meal was now discernible, with many Swiss dishes supplemented by French, Italian, and German dishes. Touches of Oriental and Caribbean cuisines made it a very enjoyable meal as I chose for the main course sesame seed–encrusted loin of lamb, duck breast with sour cherries, a pork and mushroom ragout, with the member from Aargau having a filet mignon with a Pinot Noir sauce. A Merlot from the Trentino region and a fine French Burgundy, a Pommard, were served with these.

Desserts included *zuger kirschtorte*, a rich saffron-colored cake soaked in cherry schnapps. "I would almost come here just for this," said the member as he confessed being tempted to order a second helping. We chatted for some time after the meal, then when we left the tables, twos and threes gathered in conversation with those from other tables. I saw Kathleen Evans and the new-comer, Elaine Dunbar, in a close encounter. Axel Vorstahl and Michel Leblanc were debating a culinary issue.

I talked with Oriana Frascati, and she agreed that it was a fine meal and an auspicious start to the week. Tim Reynolds, the golfer, came over. He had found a female companion from Las Vegas, where she supervised the croupiers. Margaret was a busty blonde with too much makeup but jolly and friendly. Kathleen Evans joined us as they were about to leave. "You'll be writing about this place in your column," said Reynolds.

"They keep up their standards very well," Kathleen agreed. She looked very attractive in a linen suit in a muted yellow color. "The salmon was perfect," she added, and Margaret, Tim's companion, who had had the same dish, agreed.

"You've been here before, I take it," said Margaret.

"A few times," Kathleen said, and I recalled that she had told me "once or twice."

"Well," said Tim, "we need our constitutional after that meal."

"Tim thinks twice around the grounds is a constitutional walk," said Margaret with a shudder.

"We can stop when you get tired," he said with a wink at me.

When they had left, Kathleen said, "I was thinking of a little recreation myself."

"A walk?" I offered noncommittally.

"The Seaweed Forest."

"The brochure has a picture of it. I saw one like it in a spa in Baden-Baden where the idea is said to have originated. It's a sort of flagellator—you get whipped by long lengths of seaweed as you go through."

"And did you go through?"

"No," I admitted. "It sounds medieval."

"It's very stimulating." As she said it, she turned from eavesdropping on a nearby group and gave me a full-faced stare, her eyes locked on mine.

"You must have been in it on your previous visits," I prompted.

"I'd definitely call it one of the highlights."

"Being whipped by wet seaweed . . . I don't know . . ."

Her eyes were still on mine. "You can set it to any level you want. It can be caressing, it can be restorative, it can be, as I said . . . ," she paused, ". . . stimulating." She drawled out the last word. "You should try it," she added slowly.

"I don't know what it's like until I've tried it?"

She nodded, and her lips pouted just slightly. "I'll see you there in fifteen minutes."

CHAPTER FIVE

Hydrotherapy is one of medicine's oldest curative techniques. The Greeks and the Romans believed in it firmly. The Romans found natural springs and a source of highly mineralized water in the south of England and established it as a recuperation center for the injured and war-weary soldiers of their legions. It prospered as a city, became known as Bath, and in the eighteenth century was one of the most important spas in Europe. Other European cities became known through their healing waters— Baden-Baden, Wiesbaden, Vichy, and Karlsbad, and in the United States, Colorado Springs and Battle Creek were among many spas that opened.

Despite the strong early belief in the curative powers of water, there came an inevitable backlash. How could water on the skin heal the body? skeptics asked. The attraction of the spas declined, although people still drank their water. If no other benefits were apparent, none could deny the laxative effects and this was very important in an era of overindulgence and unbalanced diets.

As the rich began to travel, they demanded more and more luxurious accommodation and a high degree of pampering. The notion of spending a portion of such travel repairing the damages done in the rest of the year sounded attractive, and the spas blossomed into temples of hedonism. "Taking the waters" became the thing to do, and eventually the medical associations of various countries undertook the study of medicinal waters. Their findings exceeded the hopes of even their most enthusiastic sponsors.

Water was found to relax and fill the blood vessels of the body, improve circulation, relieve muscle aches and spasms. Spa water, with its high content of salts, lime, magnesia, and fluorine, is many times more potent than pure water and today the spas are more popular than ever before. Spa waters are unequaled in their ability to relieve the mental and physical exhaustion resulting from the tensions of modern life.

Outside the restaurant building, I looked out across the lawn, shining softly in the rays of the sun, which was now nearing the horizon at the far end of the valley. Beyond were the buildings that housed the hydrotherapy complex. The various units were in separate edifices, large expanses of lawn between them. Most were in differing styles. Some were of wooden chalet construction, typical of Switzerland. Others were stone, some with the appearance of current design, clean, clear-cut, and in geometric shapes and some in irregular slabs with a look of the past. Others were brick with skeletons of black girders. What I was looking for was probably that mass of trees that was the nearest approximation to a forest.

"All of them help the digestion," said a voice, and one of the blond, beautiful staff members appeared.

"I'm tempted," I said. "Still trying to decide which one."

This young woman was in the identical mode as the others, smiling, friendly, and undoubtedly just as efficient. Her name tag said "Rhoda."

"The mud baths are very popular," she suggested. "But then so are the hot spring pools."

Where an Alp started its climb into the sky, I noticed a large black hole. "What's that?" I asked.

"Oh, that's the entrance to the Glacier Caverns. They are enormous chambers inside the solid ice of the glacier, and one of the natural wonders of Switzerland. They are closed to the public at the moment. The glacier is moving at the rate of several inches a year, and technicians are checking the instruments that measure it."

"So which activity do you recommend? The mud baths or the pools?"

"The mud baths are probably more popular," she said.

"I heard someone recommend the high-pressure sauna too."

She frowned. "It may be a little too vigorous so soon after eating." Then she brightened. "The Seaweed Forest might be better."

We spent several minutes discussing the various options. She knew them all well. As I had not yet tried any, the discussion was more prolonged than I would have wished. I didn't want Kathleen to become impatient and assume I wasn't coming. At last, I waved my bathing trunks and towel. "I think I'll head over there and make a decision. Thanks for your advice, er—"

From the color reproduction in the spa's brochure, it was easy to pick it out on the far side of the lawn. I set off in that direction. The air was still warm even though evening was well advanced. Only the gentlest breeze occasionally ruffled the grass, which swayed not more than a couple of millimeters in response.

It looked like a small forest as I drew near or maybe a very large thicket. Beeches, pines, and fir trees squeezed close together to form a long rectangle, probably sixty yards long and twenty yards wide, higher than a two-story house. A six-foot-high gate was the only entrance, and from it a hedge of the same height ran all around. The gate was not bolted, but after I went in I saw a sign inviting me to bolt it "if privacy is desired." I decided it was, and I did. Several cubicles were just inside the gate, and I went into the nearest and changed. Another sign stated "Wear no clothing of any kind inside the Seaweed Forest." I left my bathing trunks with my clothes and approached the "forest." Nudity is a powerful inhibitor, and I recalled that torture techniques were most effective when the victim was stripped. Why was I associating the Seaweed Flagellator with torture, I wondered? It was therapy.

Discreet notices explained the function and operation. Essentially a tunnel through the "forest," mechanical arms swung lengths of seaweed through which walked the seeker after health. They were scientifically arranged so that every part of the body except the face was chastised. A spray of warm mineral water came from above to moisten the skin. This reduced the impact of the seaweed strips and increased the excitation of the skin. At the far end, a U-turn led to a parallel return tunnel with cooler water of a different mineral content to soothe and relax the body.

A notice, which like all the others was written in English, French, and German, went on to maintain that the resultant effect was not one of flagellation but rather massage of the muscles, which was highly beneficial. It went on to describe just how beneficial, and if the notice had been written by anyone except a Swiss, it would have added "erotic." At least, I interpreted it that way, although I wondered if I was being influenced by Kathleen's invitation.

The entrance to the tunnel through the trees was a gaping hole. Subdued and hidden lights made visibility just possible but no more. I assumed that was because there was not much to see. Moisture dripped insistently from the trees, but there was no other sound. I presumed that despite my being delayed by the delightful blonde, Kathleen was not here yet.

A control panel was mounted by the tunnel entrance. Several settings were available so that one could presumably be excited to any chosen level. I was considering turning it on when I heard a sound inside, a loud rustling. Kathleen was here, after all. I plunged into the tunnel.

It was more like a jungle than a forest, warm and humid. The air had a distinct odor, obviously from the high mineral content of the water. It was a metallic sort of odor and so pervasive that I could taste it on my tongue. I had to push the seaweed strands aside to get through. When the power was on it would be easier to progress, but now the seaweed hung flaccid, almost blocking the path completely.

I called Kathleen's name, but there was no reply. I pushed on through the wet, dripping weeds, then I heard the rustling sound ahead again. She was being coy. I thrust seaweed away with both hands and went on, and suddenly she was there before me.

She was naked and leaning with her back against the seaweed flagellators. Her arms were stretched out toward me. Her eyes were closed, and her mouth was open invitingly—she did not move.

I took hold of her forearm. It was warm, but she did not respond. Her face was flushed, and I saw that the skin all over her body was livid. I lifted one eyelid gently. Her eye was cloudy, and the eyelid slid back into place.

The same sound came again, and this time it was much closer.

CHAPTER SIX

The sound came from deeper in the tunnel. It had been slightly mysterious before. Now it was threatening. I looked again at Kathleen and was reaching for her pulse when I heard what sounded like a voice. It came from the same direction as the rustling. If it was a voice, I could not distinguish any words. I was not even sure if it was male or female or what language it spoke.

No matter. I turned to Kathleen and reached for her pulse again. Just as I did so, I heard the rustling again, only this time it was immediately behind me. I started to turn, but a wave of sweetish-smelling vapor hit me in the face even as I swung around. The stuff was extraordinarily fast acting because I passed out before I could see who was behind me. Fast as it was, though, I was aware of a slight eucalyptus undertone to the odor, evidently the professional receptors working even as they lapsed into inactivity.

When I came around, it seemed like only a minute or two later. Whatever the anesthetic was, it left no aftereffects, and I was able to recall instantaneously my thoughts as I went under. My first thought now, though, was the registration of the fact that Kathleen was gone. I was sprawled against one bank of flagellators, and as I struggled upright I wondered if I had been moved and was perhaps out for longer than I had supposed. If so, maybe Kathleen was still here.

I listened carefully. All was silent. I looked for a weapon of some kind but there was nothing. I went on down the tunnel, examining every inch, but there was no sign of Kathleen. From the distance I had gone once I reached the end, I was sure I had not been moved—and if I had not, Kathleen had. There was no one here, neither her nor anyone else.

Out of the tunnel, it was already twilight. The open air was a wonderful relief after the dim, dank confines of the forest. I breathed easier, but I didn't think it safe to hang around. I grabbed my clothes and headed back to the main buildings.

The grounds were still and beautiful in the fading light. Outside the conference facility was a kiosk with two phones. I snatched the nearest, punched zero for an inside line and then eight for reception. A cool feminine voice answered.

"Get somebody out to the Seaweed Forest at once," I said, still slightly breathless. "There's been an accident."

I hung up without waiting for a reply. A low profile was the best approach until I learned more of what was happening. Switzerland was a peaceful, law-abiding country, but maybe it stayed that way by having a vigorous police force. I pulled my clothes on quickly and strolled back to the reception area as nonchalantly as I could.

Reception was a wooden Alpine building, spacious and bright. The floors were inlaid wooden tile, paintings hung on the walls, and a vast tapestry was above the enormous stone fireplace. On one side of it, a number of leather armchairs and sofas adjoined a rack of newspapers in a dozen languages. The information desk was quiet. There was only one person at the cash desk and that looked like a routine currency-changing transaction. A young man and a young woman were at the reception desk, immersed in their routine duties. All looked quite normal.

Bursting with curiosity but aware that perhaps news of a dead body had not yet hit the fan, I settled in one of the armchairs. I had sat with a copy of the *Stockholm Tagblatt* for some minutes before I remembered I did not read Swedish. I looked around the area. No one could have cared less. At the reception desk, a calm work environment continued. A phone rang and the young woman answered it, but it was evidently a guest asking a routine question.

I picked up a newspaper I could read and tried to concentrate on it. Time passed. Nothing happened. No alarm, no one rushing in disheveled to report a body, no security officers hurrying through, hastily patting their hip to make sure their sidearm was still there. I read the sports news and the fashion news and an article on the economy of the Philippines. The large clock on the wall said half an hour had now elapsed.

Certain that police would burst in at any moment, I read about electric cars and voice-actuated computers and the dwindling llama population of Peru. The time stretched out into the longest hour I could remember. Past ten o'clock, my nerves had settled but my mind was boggled. Had the staff member who took my call thought me a crank? Or was the spa so prestigious and powerful that it could gloss over a dead body? And if so, why?

I went to bed, brain still churning.

On my way to the breakfast room, I went through the reception area again. After so many hours I hardly expected to see any turmoil, and there was none. If there had been any action, it would have been during the night hours. All was orderly and tranquil, quintessentially Swiss.

Millicent Manners, princess of the soap operas, was already

at breakfast, which surprised me. I would have guessed her to be a late riser, but she explained that she was so used to being on the set early that she could not sleep past six o'clock. She used the hour after that for her daily aerobics, she said. Helmut Helberg, the supermarket king, was partway through a plateful of ham, salami, prosciutto, sausage, and three different kinds of cheese. "I like a German breakfast," he explained as he called for another cup of coffee.

To my table came a couple from Minnesota who said they were fanatical about food and were really looking forward to the classes. They were both retired schoolteachers and became involved in a long conversation with an earnest young Swiss who wrote for a newspaper in Berne and had persuaded his editor to let him cover the conference.

As far as last night's dramatic event was concerned, it had not happened. At least, there was no sign of any disturbance, no police presence, no investigative activity. The place ran as smoothly as clockwork (Swiss clockwork). Nothing ruffled the placidity, and I rattled my brains to figure out why. Had anyone been to the Seaweed Forest to check out my call? If not, had no one yet been there on a legitimate visit and run out screaming upon falling over a dead body?

Classes were due to start at nine-thirty, and I had a little preparation to do. I entered the kitchen at about nine o'clock, but I need not have worried. The ingredients were all lined up, cooking utensils were neatly laid out, burners were on low, and even so early, half a dozen eager and would-be cooks sat at desks waiting.

I put the red peppers in the oven and adjusted it to 190 degrees centigrade. The notes I had submitted on arrival had been neatly typed and gave the conversion as 375 degrees

Fahrenheit. I shelled most of the large shrimp, being careful not to remove the head and tail. I left the rest of the shrimp to be shelled as part of the demonstration. I sliced onions, covered them to keep them moist, and sliced some tomatoes.

People were drifting in now, and Caroline de Witt came in to wish me good morning. She would be introducing me, she said, and asked if there was anything else I needed. By nine-thirty, about twenty people had assembled. Caroline quickly checked names, told me all were present, and gave them my background. I was pleased to note that she concentrated on my past as a chef and made no mention of any detection activities.

I began by explaining that I was going to prepare shrimp Nissarde, a quick and easy dish but an award winner and one that permitted the imparting of a few chef's secrets. I shelled the remainder of the shrimp, pointing out that leaving on the head and tail makes for a more impressive final presentation. I took the red peppers from the oven and immediately wrapped them in newspaper. This is a trick of Provence chefs, I said. Condensation inside the paper wrapping lifts the skin away and makes the peeling process simple.

I put the sliced onions and some unpeeled garlic cloves into a bowl, then when the timer announced three minutes, I removed the newspaper and chopped the red peppers and added them. A frying pan was already warming up on a burner, and I poured in some olive oil and added the shrimp. "Be careful not to handle the shrimp too roughly, as they can easily break at any stage in the cooking," I advised.

I cooked the shrimp for two minutes, added salt and pepper, then turned the shrimp over for two more minutes. "The shrimp should now be a pale yellow-orange color," I warned, then poured in rum. "Be sure to use Barbados rum," I told them.

"The rich, heavy-bodied rums are best, as they give a more full-bodied final taste."

I touched a flame to the pan and moved the shrimp around for about fifteen seconds until the flames had almost subsided. "I am giving the pan a quick shake to extinguish the dying flames," I explained, "and make sure no combustion products remain." I removed the shrimp and added the onions, peppers, and garlic. "I am using the unshelled garlic rather than the chopped," I explained, "as it gives the dish an aroma rather than a strong garlic flavor." I added bay leaf, thyme, and rosemary, simmered a moment, and added the tomatoes and almost a cup of dry white wine.

After simmering a few minutes, the sauce had acquired a rich brown color, which I showed to the assembly. I added some basic fish sauce and simmered another two or three minutes to reduce the volume. I mixed in some fresh parsley and chervil and invited a woman from the front row to taste. She proclaimed it superb. I put the shrimp on a serving dish and poured the sauce over them.

"Finally," I said, "I'm going to drizzle some fresh olive oil over the entire mixture. When preparing tomato sauces with oil, uncooked olive oil added at the end lends a subtle freshness to the flavor."

Someone commented on how wonderful they looked, and all clamored for a taste. In five minutes, the serving platter was empty, and fresh-baked, crisp-crusted French bread was being used to mop up the remnants of the sauce.

After a few questions, I went on to mention the more exotic ways of preparing shrimp, an extremely versatile food. Piri-Piri style shrimp from Mozambique, which uses a marinade of garlic, peanut oil, and red chillies, are grilled very hot and served with a lemon butter sauce poured over them. Bengal style is cooked in a sauce of mustard, coconut, turmeric, and coriander, and Greek style with onions, tomatoes, garlic, oregano, cream sherry, and feta cheese. These mouthwatering mentions brought a flood of questions, which took us well past our eleven o'clock finishing time.

Caroline had left after watching me get well into the presentation, but she returned before the end and helped wind up what she described as a great start to the week. "I suppose you're ready for lunch after that," she commented. It was the first glint of humor I had seen from her. "I think a few lungfuls of this magnificent Alpine air is what I need," I told her. I went out into the bright sun and cogitated some more.

CHAPTER SEVEN

Cogitation was getting me nowhere. That was the only conclusion to which my cogitation brought me. Had Kathleen's body been found? Reception must have acted on my call. Someone must have gone to the Seaweed Forest, and if they had gone there, they must have found her body. Further doubt began to creep in at this point. Had she been dead? I had been feeling for a pulse when I had heard the rustling sound and the voice. Could I be certain that she was dead? Or had she recovered and hurried out?

I was reluctant to accept the latter. I recalled seeing a red danger line on the control panel. If someone had pushed the lever past that line, could the increased flagellation have caused asphyxiation?

Working with insufficient facts was not an efficient way of working. That sounded like a quote from Charlie Chan, and like most of the bons mots from the Honolulu sleuth, it had some validity. How to get more facts? Back to the reception area . . .

The young man at the desk was busy with a guest, and so I approached the young woman. Her name badge said she was Monique. "Is there a message for me?" I asked and gave her my name. She checked and came back with a sad negative. "That's strange," I said. "I had arranged to meet Kathleen Evans for lunch and I can't find her anywhere."

A slight frown creased Monique's smooth features.

"Evans . . ." She mused. "I have just seen that name." She quickly found it. "Yes, Evans, Kathleen . . . she checked out this morning."

That caught me off balance. "She couldn't have—she—" I recovered and smiled a plastic smile. "She wouldn't have left without explaining why she couldn't keep our lunch appointment." Monique looked sympathetic. "It must have been something urgent," she suggested. "But let me look again." She did so and came back with the same answer. "She definitely checked out."

"Do you have the time logged?"

She conferred with the cashier. "Six-twenty this morning."

"How did she leave? Can you find out?"

Monique nodded and picked up the phone, talked briefly. "A taxi made a pickup here at six-thirty. That must have been for Ms. Evans. She went to the airport."

I thanked her. This was getting fishier by the moment. I walked over to the travel desk. "What flights have left the airport since seven o'clock this morning?"

A large woman with a competent air answered me without even checking. "The first flight was to Frankfurt at eight. From then until noon, there have been flights to Copenhagen, Milan, Paris, Stuttgart, and Vienna."

"Can you tell me which airlines those flights were?"

"Swissair, SAS, Swissair, Air France, Lufthansa, and Swissair," she replied without hesitation. While talking, she was pushing a pad and a pencil toward me. I jotted them down and headed for the public phone outside.

It took half an hour, and at first I was Kathleen's fiancé, then I became her brother when I found that a close family member got better attention. The passenger list for the Air

France flight to Paris included the name of Kathleen Evans. Had she been on it? I persisted. The aircraft was fully loaded, I was told.

Alice was right. "Curiouser and curiouser."

It was enough to suppress one's appetite, but my life consisted of eating and activities connected with it, so I headed for the restaurant. Besides, I wanted to continue to perform normally. Did I need to? I wondered. Who might wish me harm? Whoever had killed Kathleen, was the answer, but had she been killed after all? And if so, how did she take a taxi to the airport and a flight to Paris?

As far as my involvement was concerned, no one else knew I was meeting her in the Seaweed Forest. I might have been seen but—ah! there was something. I knew of only one person who had seen me—one of the young blond staff women. True, I hadn't told her I was going to the Seaweed Forest, but all the hydrotherapy units were on the path where we had met.

I had a quick lunch—*Strudel di Fritatta*, a dish from the Italian part of Switzerland, although variations of it can be found in different regions of Italy. It is a rolled omelet with a filling of creamy goat cheese mixed with arugula. A sauce of egg yolks, cream, and a Swiss white wine helped the omelet provide some mental stimulation, or so I hoped.

At two o'clock, it was back to the schoolroom. I noticed that Marta Giannini was there, and so were Tim Reynolds, the golfer, and Elaine Dunbar, the lawyer who had made the dramatic late entrance. Michel Leblanc, the chubby chef from France, was the first speaker in the lineup.

"You must learn to prepare food before you can cook it,"

he told the class. "Preparation is mostly cutting. You must become a human food processor. You must learn to chop, slice, mince, dice—vegetables, fish, meat, poultry—all need cutting and in different ways."

He gave a demonstration with a large snapper. "Two hundred and fifty species of this fish," he said. "It's found in oceans everywhere. Every one needs cutting." He held it supported by his two hands. "Handle it only like this. A fish can bruise easier than a person." He laid it on the block and showed how to fillet it, pushing in the knife under the gill and from the backbone, slicing through it with one stroke. "Take care to remove all the bones. Filleting means 'all bones.' "

When the fish had been removed to be baked that evening. Michel went on to demonstrate poultry cutting—not carving, "that is for the table only," but cutting it into the many shapes needed for cooking. It was a fine presentation, and although I was not involved, I enjoyed sitting in the audience and absorbing it all.

The question-and-answer session was lively. One lady asked a particularly relevant question. "If I ask for a steak in a restaurant," she said, "it's reasonable that the waiter asks me how I want it cooked. But if I'm asked the same question when ordering seafood, I really don't know what to say. Surely fish should never be undercooked—isn't the risk of bacteria too high? No one wants fish overcooked. So isn't there a stage at which fish is thoroughly cooked? Then why the question?"

Michel smiled obligingly. "This is the outcome of the interest that Paul Bocuse, Alain Chapel, and other French chefs have shown in adapting features from Oriental cooking. Some diners have learned to prefer fish such as tuna and salmon cooked rare, and you have to remember also the influence of Japanese cooking. Sushi and sashimi are raw fish dishes."

"How come people who eat those in Japan don't get sick?" asked another voice.

"Within minutes of being caught, fish in Japan are flash frozen at very low temperatures, and this kills the bacteria. That is how they can serve it raw."

Caroline came in just before Michel finished. She was evidently going to all of the classes being held, and they were timed for her to have a fifteen-minute presentation between speakers and demonstrators. It was an informative quarter hour during which she covered a number of topics. She referred again to the food served at the spa. It gave the appearance, she said, of having no regard for calories, cholesterol, or fats. Nothing could be further from the truth.

Fat-free products were widely used where they did not affect taste. Yogurt replaced cream in most dishes and no one could tell the difference. White flour products and white sugar products were avoided. All breads were natural, all game was wild, and poultry was not fattened for the market. A large number of fish dishes appeared on the menus, the spa grew its own vegetables—on which no insecticides or fungicides were used—and it also grew its own herbs and spices, many of which were used in place of salt.

The presentation was something of a commercial for the spa, but it could also be used as a plan for anyone really interested in a healthy diet. Questions flooded in, and Caroline had to cut them off in order to keep to her schedule, promising to answer them all during the week. As she left, I saw Helmut Helberg, the supermarket-chain owner, come in and sit at the back of the room.

I was on next. Carver Armitage had elected to speak on shell-fish, and as the rest of the program had been formulated, I had to stay with his choice. I had already talked on shrimp, so now the topic was lobster. Two of the spiny creatures lay on the table before me.

"To kill or not to kill—that is the question," I said to start. "It's the only question—at least the lobster thinks so. But does the lobster think? If not, then perhaps it doesn't feel either. These considerations may appear more relevant to a philosophy class than a cooking class, but with loud factions defending the fox from being hunted, the whale from being caught, the bull from being fought—will the lobster be next? The state of Maine will secede from the Union first."

The smiles on some of the faces justified my diversion, and I went on to say that the most popular way of preparing a lobster dish was still to plunge the live crustacean into boiling water. Another school said using warm water and heating it to boiling was more humane. Others used a sharp knife to kill the lobster quickly, but star Paris chef Joel Robuchon was one of those who insisted that this made the meat tough. All eyes were now on the two ugly, clawed creatures on the bench in front of me.

"These were killed just before this class started, so we'll shelve the humanitarian thoughts and get back to the lobster. These two are about seven years old. This is the ideal age: they get tough after that. They weigh one and a half to two pounds. The female has more tender meat than the male. It is easy to tell the difference—the tiny legs under the tail are hard and bony on the male, soft and wispy on the female." I held them up to display this. "By the way, it's not true that lobsters are scavengers.

They eat only fresh food, preferably mussels, clams, and sea urchins."

I went on to prepare the two lobsters in front of me. The best way is probably steamed or boiled, but it can also be baked, grilled, sautéed, poached, or stir-fried. "Always use a minimum amount of water, too much takes away the flavor. Salt water is best. These two are bright red, you'll notice. They were boiled for fifteen minutes just before you arrived. Now they are cool enough to handle."

I laid each on its back and cut through the body and down the tail with a sharp knife, cutting through the underbelly but not the top shell. I flexed and drained it, cracked the claws, and drained those too. "Now I'm going to prepare these two each in a different way," I told the class. The first was baked Mediterranean style with olives, parsley, and balsamic vinegar, and the other was the classic Newburg. Both can be prepared in half an hour by interspersing the operations, and so I was able to finish them both at about the same time.

"I prepared two so that there is at least a taste of each for everybody," I said, and so there was. "Two other lobster dishes are on the menu for tonight," I added. "Pilaff and thermidor; you might want to try those."

"What's the difference between Newburg and thermidor?" someone wanted to know.

"Thermidor contains cheese, mustard, and wine, Newburg contains sherry and egg yolks. Otherwise they're the same."

It was well after five o'clock when we broke for the day. Questions were still being asked and discussions and arguments continuing, but I managed to close the class and let the students keep talking about it.

I went on another investigation.

CHAPTER EIGHT

I had a reasonably clear picture in my mind of Rhoda, the blonde who had stopped me as I had been about to set forth across the lawn last night in the direction of the hydrotherapy units. Had she really stopped me? I was not sure of that; maybe she had just happened to be there and had felt like chatting.

Another possibility was that Kathleen had only just gone to the Seaweed Forest and someone—Rhoda or someone with her—had wanted to keep me away for another quarter of an hour until . . . Until what? Until someone killed Kathleen? That might be a little fanciful, but I did not have much else, so this was worth a try.

I strolled around, passing all the buildings, walking the pathways between the cabins, going everywhere I might expect to run into one of the luscious blondes. It was Julia I wanted to see first. I knew she was not the girl I had seen last night but she could provide me with the information I needed to start. I found her taking an empty tray back to the kitchen.

"Hello, Mr. Armitage," she greeted me cheerfully. She clapped a hand to her mouth in a charming gesture. "Oh, it's not though, is it? I'm sorry, I—"

"Perfectly all right. You girls do extraordinarily well in remembering the names of the guests as well as you do. And there are so few of you . . ." I let the rest of the sentence hang in the air. She obliged.

"Eight on the day shift, five on the night shift."

"Is that all?" It was more than enough if I had to check them all out.

"We're one short today." She chattered on, bless her. "Rhoda is off. It's very short notice apparently, but something urgent came up."

I tried another approach. "You're all very photogenic. Haven't any of the magazines done a feature on you yet?"

She smiled. "Not yet. We did have a group photo taken recently though. Have you noticed it? It's in the reception."

"No, I haven't. I'll have to take a look."

When I left Julia, I hastened to the reception area as fast as I could without making my impatience obvious. The usual number of guests and staff were there, and the customary tranquillity prevailed. I picked up a newspaper and looked for a place to sit. An armchair was near, but I ignored it and walked over to another near the wall on which a large photograph was hung. I examined it. The girls looked lovely. I studied the names below and found Rhoda's.

Extreme left on the front row. I looked at the face. No doubt at all. It was the girl I had talked to on my way to the Seaweed Forest.

As we gathered before dinner, Helmut Helberg approached me. "I liked your presentation," he said. "The reason I wanted to attend was that I am thinking of having presentations like that in my markets."

I nodded. "Part of your campaign to change the supermarket image?"

"Right. It stands to reason that we could sell more lobsters if people knew more about them—how to buy them, how to prepare them."

"The public is more afraid of the lobster than of any other food," I said. "It has a terrifying appearance for a start. Most people don't know what to look for and don't know how to prepare it."

"A lot of customers don't want to be bothered to prepare it," Helberg argued.

"Then you should consider preparing it for them."

"But they don't keep."

"On-the-spot preparation—prepared to order. While still fresh."

He took on a pensive look and wandered away. I had a short conversation with Oriana Frascati. "Getting any ideas for your cookbooks?" I asked. She was not unattractive but used no makeup, and her hair looked as if it had not spent much time under the care of a hairdresser.

"Too many," she sighed. "I already have a full schedule for the winter and the manuscripts keep flooding in."

"Must be hard to find new approaches," I suggested.

She studied me as if trying to decide whether to confide in me. "I have several possibilities," she murmured. "I'm doing some final sifting right now. Maybe you would like to give me your opinion on them?"

"Pleased to," I said, and waited. She nodded as if satisfied. "I'll be talking to you," she said, and walked off. They must be confidential, I thought, and she is afraid that the competition will hear about them. Was the cookbook business as cutthroat as the rest of the publishing business? I wondered.

Caroline de Witt was there, looking glamorous in a tight-fitting black dress. I congratulated her. "Superb organization," I told her. "Everything is running as smoothly as—well, as a Swiss watch."

She smiled appreciatively. "Thank you. It's a lot of work but very rewarding."

"An eclectic group of students too."

"Yes. Classes like this are very gratifying. The interest is not professional in a direct sense but just as intense. It is more diverse, it brings in so many other concerns. The people are more demanding."

"Your facilities are very impressive," I said. "I haven't had a chance yet to partake of them all—"

"Oh, you must," she implored, laying a beautifully mani-cured hand on my arm. "The mud baths—"

"Yes, I want to try those first. Then there are the oth-ers. . . ."

"The underground sauna is wonderful, so beneficial. The Seaweed Forest too is so healthful."

"Hmm," I tried to sound reluctant. It was not difficult. "Sounds dangerous to me. More of a jungle than a forest, some-body said. It's a flagellator, isn't it?"

She laughed musically. "Oh, yes, but a very gentle one."

An image floated into my mind of a dead body among those "gentle" seaweed strands. "You really must try it," she insisted.

I nodded, still reluctant.

"I will see how my schedule is. Maybe I can introduce you to it."

"That would be nice," I said politely. My last assignation with a female in the Seaweed Forest was not a situation I wanted to repeat.

———

The dinner menu did indeed include the two lobster dishes I had mentioned, but a couple of other items caught my eye. For a starter, I chose the Cuban tamales, a dish containing pork, a Cuban favorite, and served with a sauce of orange, cherry, and lime juices with onion and garlic. The tamales had a pleasantly fragrant herbal taste that was unusual, and when I asked I was told that it was "culentro," a Central American variant of coriander and much stronger.

Brad Thompson, the fast-food millionaire, was at my table and displaying an enterprising spirit in ordering the chilled zucchini bisque. A large baked zucchini blossom floated on the surface, stuffed with goat cheese and diced tomatoes.

For the main course, I selected a Swiss dish on the basis that it is hard to find outside of Switzerland. This was Egli, a variety of perch, delicate in flavor, white, and almost without bones. Brad Thompson had a grilled paillard of beef. It was served with red cabbage, a popular vegetable in Switzerland, and a red wine sauce fortified with port. A light fresh white wine from the Saar Valley went well with my fish. Brad chose a Cote Rotie to accompany his beef, and although I thought he might find it sufficiently full-bodied but too scented, I heard no complaints. He concluded with a peanut butter mascarpone, and I had a peach sorbet.

I slipped out as smoothly as I could. Caroline de Witt was only two tables away, and while I was determined to solve the mystery of the Seaweed Forest, I was not prepared to attempt it right now. The right mind-set would be critical, I told myself.

CHAPTER NINE

I was still curious about Leighton Vance. My schedule to date had been such that my presentations had coincided with his, so I had not had the opportunity to observe him in action. The next morning I was free, and I saw that he was giving a demonstration in conference room C. After a breakfast of fresh mango juice, some muesli made in the original style of Doctor Bircher-Brenner (who had lived near here), Nicaraguan coffee, and fresh-baked wheat rolls, I went to sit at the feet of the guru of Swiss cuisine.

My attitude was admittedly a little snide, considering how he had thrown me out of his kitchen—which was the way I persisted in thinking of it. So I sat in the second row—not the first, where I would be staring him in the face, and not in the back row, where I could toss in unexpected lobs of awkward questions. I wanted to keep it fair but still hold an advantage.

"More than a third of all new chefs are career changers," he began. "That in itself is a clear indication of the attraction that cooking possesses. Learning to cook means cooking every-day dishes as well as those for special occasions.

"In recent years, chefs have been challenged by the addition of a new dimension. No longer is a meal expected only to look good and taste good: it must be healthy. Some dishes were immediately struck off the cooking list because they were too high in calories or fats. Pork was among the first to go."

It was a good start, I conceded. A controversial topic was being introduced now.

"Containing less protein and more fat than other meats, pork requires cooking at a hundred and sixty degrees Fahrenheit minimum to kill the trichinae, the bacteria that cause trichinosis. This rule was not always observed in the past and thus gave pork a bad name.

"Today, lean cuts of pork are similar in both fat content and dietary cholesterol to chicken breasts. They contain greater amounts of thiamin and other vitamins and by minimizing the amount of oil used for cooking, you can eat pork without guilt."

Leighton indicated two pork tenderloins before him. "I am going to barbecue these in a Chinese style, with garlic sauce," he said. "The oven is already preheated at three hundred and fifty degrees, and this baking pan is lined with foil." He whisked together hoisin sauce, garlic, ketchup, sugar, and soy sauce. He put the tenderloins in the pan, coated them with this mixture, and put them in the oven.

"I am going to cook these for thirty-five minutes," he said, "but before the class started I put two identical tenderloins in. These will be due out in five minutes, and in the meantime I am going to make the garlic sauce." He stirred together soy sauce, minced garlic, vinegar, sugar, and a sprinkle of Tabasco sauce, then warmed the mixture in a small pan, took the pre-cooked tenderloins out of the oven, and placed them on a cutting board. He cut them diagonally across the grain into thin slices and poured the sauce over them.

"Come and try them," he said invitingly, and there was a rush. "Only about one hundred and thirty calories an ounce and two and a half grams of fat." When the pork had vanished, he

said, "Now, while the other tenderloins are cooking. I'm going
to show you how to make a typical Chinese accompaniment in
order to serve a well-rounded meal. This is stir-fried vegetables
with noodles."

He took onions, broccoli, leeks, and carrots and steamed
them for two or three minutes. He put noodles into boiling
water—the so-called rice stick-noodles also known as rice ver-
micelli—and drained them when they were tender, which took
about ten minutes. For a sauce, he mixed soy, Bourbon whiskey,
and chicken broth with cornstarch, sugar, salt, and sesame oil.
In a small pan, he sauteed ginger and garlic with curry powder
and turmeric. He added the vegetables and the noodles and
stirred.

"Bring plates," he told the class as he opened the oven and
began to slice the pork tenderloins. "This time, you can taste the
whole dish."

The presentation was a great success, and I told him so. He
gave me a curt nod and turned his attention to Millicent Manners. The soap opera actress was giving him starry-eyed looks,
and their conversation was carried on in lowered tones. It did
not sound as if they were talking about food.

The tastes of barbecued pork tenderloin, garlic sauce, and a mixture of noodles and vegetables had been delicious, but they had
given me an appetite. I was early for lunch and selected a cheese-
and-onion salad, a specialty from the Appenzell in the north-
western corner of Switzerland, where Austria and Lake
Constance come together. Maintaining continuity, I followed it
with *siedfleischteller*, a type of beef stew from the same region.

Helmut Helberg came to the table, perspiring slightly.

"The underground sauna," he explained, "it's wonderful. Makes you perspire and lose all those body poisons. The trouble is I can't stop!"

"Do you find it helps the thought processes?" I asked. "Did you get all kinds of great ideas for the reformation of the supermarket?"

"A few," he admitted cautiously. I supposed the grocery business must be susceptible to industrial espionage in the same way as many others.

He scanned the menu and sighed. "So many choices."

"I went for Swiss dishes," I said, and told him what they were. He accepted my recommendation on the Appenzeller beef stew but wanted a more substantial dish to start. He stayed true to national tastes and ordered a warm potato salad with chopped onion, ham, green pepper, and mustard.

"Does the territory covered by your supermarket chain include Switzerland?" I asked.

"Certainly."

"I was thinking that it's a pity Swiss chefs are not better known outside their own country."

"That's true," he agreed. He had ordered a glass of red wine. It arrived and he sipped and nodded approval.

"Through your business, you must know some of these chefs. Fredy Girardet has become almost a legend, but perhaps it is his eminence that has kept other Swiss chefs from being recognized."

"Martin Dalsass at the Sant'abbondio in the Ticino is outstanding," he said promptly. "He is also a good friend of mine. Then there is Waldis Ratti. He has the Ristorante Rodolfo on the shore of Lake Maggiore. Horst Peterman in Zurich is growing quickly in stature, and so is Hans Stucki in Basel."

"Outside of Switzerland, we don't hear enough of these names," I said. "Peterman is becoming well known, though."

We discussed Swiss cooking and the influence on it of German cooking, but when the food arrived, Helmut gave full attention to it and slowed down in his conversation.

As we left, I encountered Marta Giannini, resplendent in a burgundy-colored dress of some shimmering material. "Have you tried the mud baths here yet?" she asked.

"Not yet, but they're high on my list," I told her.

"I just love the mud baths at the Gellert in Budapest," she said, using those magnificent eyes as if cameras were focused on her from all angles. "The Romans began the tradition there, you know. It was the Turks, though, who converted them into the way they are today."

"I don't know how old these are," I confessed. "The Romans were certainly in this region. But I'm sure the mud is new."

"Are you taking a class this afternoon?"

"Only a short one at four o'clock."

"Then perhaps I'll see you there." The luminous eyes were irresistible. I agreed.

CHAPTER TEN

The entrance to the mud baths was dark from the outside, but that was a trick of the glittering sun. Inside, the bath was lit with bulbs like giant pumpkins that gave off a soft natural light. A winding path led inward and soon merged into a vast subterranean palace with a low roof of natural glistening rock.

Bronze fittings on the lamps gave it a period look, but the earth-brown marble of the mud bath was clearly modern. In it, rich brown mud heaved and bubbled, sending clouds of steam wafting into the humid atmosphere.

One of the lovely blond staff girls was on duty. I had not seen her before. This one looked like the star of the Olympic swimming team. Her tiny bikini allowed no space for a name badge, and she introduced herself with, "I'm Celia."

In the simmering bath of mud, three vaguely human shapes could be distinguished, wallowing gently like grotesque sea creatures. I had to reach the side of the bath before I could identify a couple from Dublin whom I had met in the restaurant. I turned my attention to the third figure and was just able to make out the features of Marta Giannini. Her eyes sparkled out of the thick gelatinous mass that parted reluctantly as she raised a hand to wave.

I slid in beside her. It was different from what I had expected. Instead of getting into the mud, all I could do at first was lie on top. It was denser and heavier than it looked, like a

mass of unbaked pumpernickel dough. Gradually I began to settle, sinking very, very slowly. Marta laughed, and the sound
tinkled and echoed from the low ceiling.

"Don't think about your nose itching! If it does, you will
want to rub it and then you have a problem!"

"I won't think about it." It was an impossible promise.

"You're an old hand at this mud bath venture, aren't you?"

"I love them," she said gleefully.

I floated for a while. I thought I was sinking deeper very
slowly but my face was still above the mud.

"This isn't just ordinary mud," Marta said. "The mineral
water from the natural springs deep down makes it different,
gives it medicinal powers. It's wonderful for the skin."

"Does anybody ever sink?" I asked.

"The mineral water being pumped in has a very strict temperature control on it. That keeps the mud at just the right consistency."

Right for what? I wondered. It was too dense to swim in
and too thin to float on. I moved my arms and it was frustratingly
difficult. I kicked but nothing happened. The Irish couple was
climbing out, saying something to Marta. She smiled and I
thought she nodded but the movement was minimal. Celia led
the couple into a shower cubicle and handed them white terrycloth robes. They left, and Marta called to me, "Still afloat?"

"I think so. Is my skin peeling yet?"

She laughed, expert enough in mud bathing to prevent
mud from slipping into her mouth. I lay there, immobile. It was
like being suspended in space and after the passage of an inde-
terminate number of minutes, suspended in time too.

A loud piercing noise broke my reverie. It was a while
before I recovered full consciousness, and I became aware that

the blond girl was talking to Marta. The piercing noise stopped, and I saw the cell phone in the blond Celia's hand. Marta moved slowly, slowly to the side of the pool. She pulled herself half out and turned to me. Venus arising from the mud bath, I thought.

"My agent and an executive from Universal are on a conference call," she said. "They want to talk to me about a new part. I'll have to take it in my room."

"Good luck," I wished her sincerely. Celia helped her out and took her to the shower. Marta gave me a wave as she disappeared. Celia came back to the edge of the bath. "I have to go and look at the temperature. I'll be right back."

"All right," I managed to say.

"I'm not supposed to leave you alone," she said, "but I'll only be a minute or two."

She walked away with a sway of the hips that was so different from any of those I had seen before. I went back into my mud world.

I was exfoliating. My skin was coming off in huge patches. Soon I was going to be a hunk of unprotected flesh, grotesque and unrecognizable. I would submerge in a hot steamy swamp and be lost.

Consciousness began to seep back slowly. Relief flooded my mind. I couldn't see any of my skin, but I knew it was not peeling. That had been just one of the fears implanted easily because of my negligible knowledge of mud baths. I was not submerging either—that was just another fear that . . .

But I *was* submerging. My nose and mouth were barely above the brown ooze. It *was* hot now, hotter than when I had gone in and so steamy that I could hardly see the stone ceiling. I tried to move my arms and legs but it was not possible.

The steamy air parted as a figure came through it, coming into focus like an image at a séance. It must be Celia returning . . . but no. The blond girls looked very much alike, but surely this wasn't Celia. The steam swirled, the face came and went. I tried to gasp out a plea for help, but I could hear no words emerging. She was looking down at me. Why didn't she help me? I must have passed out from the heat, and when my eyelids had struggled apart I was first aware of the effort to move them and then of the fact that the face had gone.

I was aware again of the temperature of the mud. It was getting hotter by the minute. It must have been acting as a soporific, for I drifted off into a hazy world of only one sensation—heat. It was lulling my brain into a stupor, and even the effort of trying to formulate a thought was too much.

Through the haze of unreality, I had the panicky feeling that I was sinking deeper and deeper, slow though it was. My limbs did not exist, or if they did I no longer had any control over them. Breathing was getting more difficult, I suddenly realized. The moist air was heavy and cloying and my lungs did not want to make the effort. The mud was seeping into my ears, and I thought I could hear a faint glug-glug of bursting bubbles. But the sound was attenuated, as if stretched by the heaving mud.

The awareness of the need for survival was still there, though. A tiny stirring in the back of my mind was urging me to do something, anything, to escape from this world of heat and humidity where the least movement required massive effort, and time seemed to be moving at a cosmic crawl.

The thought crept in as to whether I would ever come back from such a world.

———

I had no recollection of forcing my eyes open and yet another face was filling my vision. Was I dreaming? Was I still in a universe of increasingly unbearable heat? Was that the sound of a muffled voice, calling out incomprehensible words?

Like successive shots in a film, actuality returned. First steamy white air, then undulating thick mud all around me, then the marble edge of the pool. Marta was trying to pull me out of the mud, and it was reluctant to let me go. My head emerged, and even the heavy humid air felt cool by comparison. The heat still enveloped the rest of my body, and in a moment of sheer irrelevance I resolved to review the matter of lobsters and boiling water.

I could see Marta clearly now. She was struggling to pull me free of the clinging mud, but she was not strong enough. I was slipping back but recovering just enough to be trying to kick and struggle when a blond vision appeared. She and Marta heaved me out as if beaching a large and exhausted fish. I flopped on to the cool marble.

The blond girl was strong and muscular. She half carried me into the shower cubicle, and fresh clear water had never felt so good. She handed me a plastic mug of sparkling water with slices of cucumber, chunks of lemon, and ice. It tasted wonderful, and she filled the mug again from a large pitcher. I dropped into the nearest chair.

Marta was at my side, looking concerned. She was wearing a white terrycloth robe, spattered with mud from her attempts to pull me out. "Drink some more," said the blond girl, filling my mug again. "It will replace the moisture. You must have lost a lot."

"You saved my life," I said to both of them. "What's your

name?" I asked the blond girl. She wore only a bikini as brief as that of the previous girl.

"Anita," she replied. "Where is Celia?"

"She went to adjust the temperature," I said as normality crept back. "She must have misread the dial or got hold of the wrong handle.

"Can you bring me one of those robes?" I asked. Now that I was feeling better, nudity seemed out of place.

Anita brought me a robe. "I'll have a look at the temperature control," she said, and disappeared into the steam haze.

Marta gave me a brief, reassuring smile. "It's a good thing I came back. What happened to you?"

"The pool got hotter. I got weaker. I passed out. I hope this never happened to you at the Gellert."

"Mud baths are supposed to be invigorating," she said.

"This one wasn't," I told her, and sat for a few minutes as my strength returned.

"This must remind you of *Shanghai Nights*," I told her. "You ran an establishment with a very doubtful reputation. You fell in love with the chief of police, who had to put you out of business or the politicians would get him fired. He stood up to them, they had him hit on the head and thrown into the Pacific and you saved him—you had been standing on the pier where you were going to drown yourself."

"Ah yes, Josef—he was a great director. He fell in love with me during that picture."

"I thought your costar, Robert what's his name, fell in love with you in that picture?"

She smiled wistfully. "Yes, Robert too—but it was Lloyd I married."

"I thought that was Kent?"

"He was next."

We laughed together. "I think you have recovered," she said, "and at least the hot mud hasn't softened your brain. Do you remember all my movies?"

"Every single one," I said—one of the rare occasions on which I think it permissible to lie is when talking to a beautiful woman.

Anita came back frowning. "The temperature control is set for normal, but the thermometer reading is fifteen degrees higher."

"I would have been cooked like a goose in another few minutes," I told her.

She was still frowning. "I don't understand. The control must have been running under a higher setting for a period of time. I must report this. It is a very serious matter."

"I agree. I'm glad you arrived when you did."

"I was not supposed to relieve Celia for another half hour," she said. "You are lucky I came early."

Marta walked back to the main buildings with me. She could pass for twenty years younger, I thought. She was still a very beautiful woman—and not just because she had saved my life. That reminded me . . .

"Thanks again for saving my life," I said.

"Anytime," she said, then looked at me anxiously. "No, I didn't mean that. I hope it doesn't happen again."

The grass was soft and the air clean and pure. It was good to be alive.

Marta said almost to herself, "I wonder how the temperature got up that high."

She surprised me. I had thought of her as being totally self-absorbed. I was glad to be wrong.

It was a point that I had started to think about now that the shock had worn off. It might not have been so significant, but this was the second time that one of the blond staff members had been involved—the first time in a death (or at least an unaccountable disappearance) and the second time in a near death. From now on, I was going to look at those girls with suspicion. How many more of them could be involved?

"There's another thing," Marta said. "I didn't think it had any meaning before, but now . . ."

"Go on," I encouraged her.

"I waited a long time on that phone line. I was told to wait, wait. . . . Finally, a voice said there was a problem with the line and they would try again later."

"It's possible," I said. "Even Swiss telephones aren't perfect."

"I called my agent in New York. He knew nothing about a conference call." I was silent. She continued, "He is trying to put together a deal for a new picture, but it's not ready yet."

"Yes, that is strange," I admitted. "Some kind of mistake, I suppose."

"It must have been."

She might have been waiting for me to tell her that I was in the Secret Service and could not tell her any more. She had probably heard that line in half a dozen movies, although that would not mean she was ready to believe it now. I thought of telling her more, but at this stage I did not want to get her involved. I was not sure yet of what was happening. All I knew was that too much of it was happening to me.

I could always quit and go back to London.

No, I couldn't. I was really curious, and besides, I liked the spa. I would hang in there a little while longer, even if I didn't have a paying client—and even if someone did want to boil me like . . . well, like a lobster.

CHAPTER ELEVEN

I had no time to reflect on my narrow escape from being boiled to death—an inexcusable end for a gourmet detective. Our session at four o'clock began right on time—always a predictable occurrence in Switzerland.

Four of us were on the podium—Leighton Vance, Michel Leblanc, Axel Vorstahl, and I. Caroline introduced us and pointed out again that the week's classes and demonstrations were not basically for professionals. A few of these attended, those who wanted to brush up or those who had been away from cooking for some time. Basically, though, the classes were for serious amateurs or those in auxiliary fields.

"The latter includes guests that the spa is pleased to have with us this week," said Caroline. She named Oriana Frascati as an editor of cookbooks, Helmut Helberg as the owner of a supermarket chain, and Bradley Thompson as a fast-food pioneer.

"This is to be a short session," she explained. "You will all have accumulated a lot of questions so far, and many may not have had the opportunity to have them answered in the regular classes. So here is your chance. . . ."

It was a popular idea, and the room was crowded. Questions came thick and fast. First of all, someone wanted to know what to do about salt. "We are supposed to cut down on it—in the United States, the federal government says by at least one-third. Salt contributes to high blood pressure, we are told. But everyone knows that there is just no substitute for salt when it comes to flavor. What is the answer?"

Michel Leblanc fired the first shot. "The desire for salt comes when a society moves away from fresh foods to processed foods. Unfortunately, all processed foods contain extremely high amounts of sodium, added as a preservative." He turned an apologetic face to Helmut Helberg and he answered promptly.

"Bradley and I are, of course, suppliers of processed foods, and we must use preservatives so that canned foods have the shelf life that customers demand."

Caroline, presiding, was cleverly bringing in all the members of the panel as early and as quickly as possible. She pointed next to me.

"Salt is trapped in a vicious circle," I said. I wanted to avoid taking up the cudgels on behalf of either of the proponents here. "As the body craves more salt, the demand grows for saltier foods, such as prosciutto, cheese, olives, potato chips, dried beef, canned fish, frankfurters, canned soups—"

"Aren't there other preservatives besides salt?" someone chipped in.

Caroline's imperious finger swung to Leighton Vance. "Certainly," he said. "First, though, I must emphasize that life as we know it could not exist without preservatives. We would have to go back to the Stone Age. Chemical preservatives are by far the cheapest kind—"

"—and salt is the cheapest of all," contributed Helmut.

As the finger swiveled in my direction, I was ready. "Other methods include heating, chilling, freezing, fermentation, pickling, smoking . . . Irradiation may turn out to be the most efficient, but there is customer resistance to any link between food and nuclear radiation, and even the best PR people haven't solved that problem yet."

"Perhaps we should get back to the original question," said Caroline smartly. "It really asked, How can the chef avoid salt?" The discussion flowed. Use more pepper, use paprika, use lemon juice, use mustard or fresh basil or thyme—all were proposed. The final word came from Oriana Frascati. "If you must use salt, make it kosher salt—it's the purest and the only one free of objectionable chemicals."

A question came on a different subject. "I'm redesigning my kitchen at home. I do a lot of entertaining, so what are the most important points to bear in mind?"

Axel Vorstahl was first to tackle that one. He had worked with kitchen designers on land as well as on cruise ships, he said. Modifying this experience for a personal kitchen, he made the following suggestions: have lots of open shelving and glass-fronted cupboards; have a refrigerator under the counter and put a freezer in the pantry; treat all countertops with polyurethane for the best resistance to bacteria; capture as much natural light as you can and have halogen lighting tracks to augment it; have heat and water close together by having a faucet adjacent to the cooktop.

"What do you think about uncooked food?" was another query. "Some health clinics prescribe raw foods for better health."

All four of us commented on this. Helmut Helberg pointed out that cooking actually increases the nutritional content of several vegetables, including carrots and tomatoes. That steaming is always better than boiling was universally agreed.

"We're getting bored with French cooking, Italian

cooking, Chinese food . . . ," called a voice. "When are we going to get something new, something different?"

There was a pause, and Caroline looked at us all in turn before I ventured an answer. "What about Russian cooking? It has a lot of potential that hasn't yet been tapped in the West. Maybe it will be next." Some discussion followed, but no one had any better ideas. Indonesian and Philippine cooking were mentioned, but many thought them only variations on Chinese.

More inquiries flowed, with Helberg, Frascati, and Thompson contributing as much as those of us on the panel. Vance had the least to say. He seemed to have something on his mind. When we finally broke up, a man of the audience wanted to pursue points with selected panelists, and our "short" session became as long as the others.

When I finally left the conference room, I looked for a blond staff girl—any of them. The first one I encountered was Helga, according to her name badge. "Is Celia still on duty?" I asked.

"I think she's still on mud bath duty," she responded with a smile.

I went there with a cautious tread, but it appeared safe as half a dozen people were lolling in the thick brown mud and others were coming in. Celia was there and greeted me with a smile.

"I was in the mud bath earlier today," I told her.

"Oh yes, of course. I remember." She looked at my stern expression. "Is something wrong?"

"Yes, I almost drowned."

"In the mud?" she said, sounding unconvinced.

"You left me, saying you were going to adjust the temperature. You adjusted it too much—I almost boiled."

I studied her carefully. There was no trace of guilt as she said, "I raised it one degree only." Her brown eyes looked quite innocent. I pressed her further. "You said you'd be back in a minute or two. You didn't return at all."

She shook her head. "I had a message to say that I was to report for room service duty and that Anita was replacing me earlier than scheduled."

"Anita did come early, luckily for me. I might have been dead."

She was either a wonderful actress or quite blameless. "I am so sorry but I was only obeying instructions. I had no idea . . ." The blond hair danced as she shook her head again. "I cannot understand how the temperature could get that high. I will have the maintenance department look at it."

I left her, a bikini-clad figure standing in the steamy chamber. If she was telling the truth, someone else had arranged the whole incident and turned up the temperature. I recalled Marta's episode with the phone call that never came through. Had that been part of the scheme too, making sure I was alone?

Considered in isolation, it might have been an unusual collection of coincidences, but coming after my discovery of Kathleen's dead body in the seaweed flagellator, the coincidence factor was too high. Assuming that she had really been dead, of course.

She must have been, I decided. That raised questions of who had taken the body—and where—and why. Further investigation was needed. That raised even more questions—like what—and how—and when. This place had become a mass of puzzles.

CHAPTER TWELVE

A refreshing gin and tonic before dinner helped a little. At the dining table, I was seated with a doctor with a passion for cooking, a retired airline pilot from Swissair who was thinking of opening a restaurant, an American couple now living in Spain, and our most recent arrival, the lady lawyer, Elaine Dunbar. She was already debating the legal rights of airline passengers with the pilot, who was beginning to bristle with all the chauvinism of a country that still didn't really think that women had any right to be voting.

I started with the pancetta and artichoke fettucine, a Swiss-Italian dish. Again, I had to compliment the chef. He had used egg fettucine, which is much thinner and lighter than the regular kind. The artichokes had had their leaves carefully trimmed. The pancetta—bacon, cured but not smoked—had been cooked till just crisp, while garlic and wine accentuated the flavor.

The German part of Switzerland was represented among the main courses by lamb shank braised with red cabbage, and again Leighton Vance had performed outstandingly. A more earthy, peasant type of dish like this needed a wine with similar characteristics, and I selected a Château de Pibarnon, a red Bandol made from the Mourvedre grape. After some conversation at the table, I decided to go and congratulate him in person.

In the kitchen, busboys were still bringing in dishes and loading them directly into the washers. One sous-chef was scrub-

bing the wooden chopping boards and another—it was Mallory—was writing on a pad. She looked up, startled, then smiled
when she saw it was me. "Making a list for tomorrow," she
explained.

No one else was there, and the kitchen was beginning to
acquire the weary but satisfied look of an establishment that has
done its work for the day. "I came to congratulate Leighton on
the meal," I told her, and described the dishes.

She dimpled and looked pleased. "I'll tell him," she said.

"What are your specialties?" I asked.

"Specialties?"

"What do you like to cook?"

"Oh, all kinds of dishes."

"Swiss, French, German?"

"Yes, and Italian too. I love Oriental cooking and learning
how their methods can be fused with ours."

We talked about specific dishes, and she revealed a well-
rounded knowledge. She must be a great help as a sous-chef and
I told her so. "I love it," she said enthusiastically.

We talked further, but she was becoming increasingly edgy
and casting furtive glances at the door. I gathered that she was
nervous that Leighton would return and repeat his earlier performance of throwing me out of his kitchen. I did not want to
see her embarrassed, so I told her I'd talk to her again when she
wasn't so busy.

"I'm always busy," she replied, then added quickly, "but
please come again."

One of the larger lounges was popular after meals, and at
the door I met Elaine Dunbar. She was wearing a slightly severe
light gray checked suit, which she probably considered appropriate attire for a lawyer.

"You're Armitage, aren't you?" she said.

"A popular misconception but an understandable one." She hadn't been paying attention when we had been introduced by Caroline upon the occasion of her dramatic entrance, but she had met a number of new people. I explained why I was not Armitage.

"Have you been here before?" she asked.

"I haven't been in a spa before."

"Neither have I."

"I imagine that this is as good a place as any to get the atmosphere and the feel of cooks, cooking, and food," I told her. "Just what you are looking for."

We took a large leather settee with a long table and ordered caffe lattes. "What am I looking for?" she asked, her voice just short of aggression.

"You're looking for interfaces between the food and restaurant business on the one hand and the law on the other."

"Something like that," she said dismissively.

"I thought it a pretty good summary from what you told us when you arrived."

Her profile was more attractive than her full-front view, I decided. It avoided the bold, somewhat dominant appearance that she displayed when viewed full face. This latter aspect would probably be valuable in a courtroom, though.

"People in the food and restaurant business that I have talked to so far have much too simplistic a viewpoint on their own position. They think everybody in the trade is kind and friendly and helpful. They refuse to see all the corruption and fraud that surround them."

"And those are what you are going to seek out?"

"Did you know that in the United States, over a hundred million cases of food-related illnesses are reported every year?"

"Salmonella in chicken and eggs, undercooked ground beef, fish that are caught in polluted waters, fruit that have been oversprayed with pesticide," I said. "But I didn't realize the number was that high."

"It's higher in Europe, and food poisoning is only a start. Olestra is keeping batteries of law firms busy, and it's only one of a great many fat substitutes that everybody wants because it's easier than dieting yet causes severe intestinal problems in certain people. Now that the beef business is under close scrutiny, we can expect lots of legal cases from it."

"Especially since the Oprah Winfrey case?" I said.

"Of course. She had the money to go to court, but for every Oprah there are hundreds of people out there with cases that could be just as sound."

"Those are the ones you are going to represent?"

"Why not? Shouldn't someone?" She was getting more vehement, so I stepped up my pace too.

"Are you going to tell me that the public needs protecting against dangerous foods and you believe it to be your mission to be their standard-bearer?"

Her face tightened, and I prepared myself for an onslaught. Instead, she laughed softly and leaned back, a woman now and less the lawyer. "No. I have no pretensions toward being a crusader."

"Or even the Joan of Arc of the hamburger world riding fearlessly into the slaughterhouses?"

"Not even that," she said, still smiling. "There are so many other areas where more legal participation is needed. In both

Europe and the U.S., more than half of all the drugs approved annually are known to have serious post-approval risks. And then there's advertising in which the interpretation of a single word could have catastrophic consequences for the consumer and for pharmacies and health food stores."

"So it's the prospect of myriad challenges that you relish?"

"And in an almost virgin field," Elaine insisted. "A field that has been virtually overlooked."

"Do you have any particular case in mind? I mean, have you been retained to undertake one such case?"

"I don't have my shingle hanging out there yet. I will after I've spent a week here, though, and know more what I'm getting into."

Our caffe lattes arrived. Elaine stirred hers and gazed into the milky depths. "In the final year of my doctorate, I did run across one case . . ."

"Aha, I knew it."

"Oh, it influenced me, no doubt about that, but I had already decided that this was what I wanted to do in the practice of law. No, this particular case involved food poisoning, as a matter of fact, but it was in a restaurant. A lot of ramifications came into play and are still coming into play."

"Still coming into it? The case is still on?"

"It's being reopened." She picked up her cup and sipped. "That's why I probably shouldn't be talking about it."

"Will you be getting involved in this case when you open your practice? It sounds intriguing."

"I don't know. I'd like to get involved in it, but I don't know."

"It sounds as if there are personal aspects that attract you as much as the concept and the potential crime."

She looked at me over her coffee cup.

"They do, and a lot more is to be revealed, perhaps very soon."

The caffe latte was smooth. As I was taking the first sips, Elaine asked, "You are a detective of some kind, aren't you? I recall now that when I came in and Caroline introduced us, she did say that Carver Armitage had to cancel and you were replacing him. What did she call you?"

" 'The Gourmet Detective.' It's just a nickname. I'm not a detective at all. I hunt for rare foods, seek out unusual food ingredients, advise on applications—that kind of thing."

"It's detecting in a way, isn't it?"

"Only very peripherally. Oh, assignments sometimes take nasty turns, but most of the time it's just an interesting but routine job."

"Did you know any of the people here before you came?" I asked.

"No, none of them."

We discussed several of the guests. Elaine showed a lively curiosity about all of them. "Professional interest?" I asked. She considered for a moment.

"It could turn out that way—very easily," she said.

Elaine had some work to do, she told me briskly. I asked her if she was doing some pre-practice work. "In a way," she answered. "A friend from law school is now practicing, and I'm helping her build a case. It's the kind of case that I'm going to go for, so this is good preparation for me."

"You mean it's something to do with food?"

"Helen—this friend—is suing the city where she lives for supplying substandard water."

"How does the city get away with that?" I asked.

"There are guidelines for water quality, but it is up to each water authority to enforce them."

"And this city isn't enforcing them?"

"Independent analyses have shown that the water does not meet federal guidelines. The city says the water meets state requirements and that is their first responsibility."

"So the federal authorities should be putting pressure on the state."

"They claim they are. In the meantime, an increase in spinal meningitis points a finger at the boron in the water. People are dying while bureaucrats argue whose responsibility takes priority."

"Sounds to me like you're taking on some tough opposition," I remarked.

Her teeth gleamed. It was a smile that suggested the opposition could expect some tough times too.

When she had gone, I sat for a while. Finally, one of the blond staff girls walked by, and I raised a hand to attract her attention. She was just as attractive as the others and her name was Anna, her badge declared.

"Tell me, Anna, where is Rhoda? I haven't seen her around."

"She's off for a few days. She should be back soon." The girl smiled.

It sounded like a stock answer.

"She's not ill, I hope," I went on, trying to get something out of her.

"Oh, no, just some personal business, I think." About to walk away, she added, "It leaves us a little short-handed."

She walked away with that swinging gait that was typical

of all of them. The gaits were not all exactly the same, though. With a little study, they could be used to identify the owner. More to the immediate point, though—the absent Rhoda who might know something about the attempt on my life in the mud bath and possibly Kathleen's disappearance was not available for questioning.

It was not evidence, but it was certainly suspicious.

CHAPTER THIRTEEN

The topic at the breakfast table the next morning was the perennial one of Swiss neutrality. Karl Wengen, the representative on the national council of the canton of Aargau, was at my table, and it was inevitable that someone should ask the question that the Swiss hear every day.

"How has Switzerland managed to remain neutral for centuries?" asked Bradley Thompson. As befitted a person who had built up a business virtually single-handedly, Brad was never shy about asking provocative questions.

"Four centuries, in fact," Karl Wengen said. "It is four hundred years since we were involved in a war."

"It's so improbable," protested an earnest Japanese lady with severe-looking spectacles and shiny black hair. She went on, "You are surrounded by warring countries—Germany, France, Italy, Austria—and yet Switzerland remains aloof. What is your secret?"

"No secret," smiled Wengen. "Surrounded by other countries, as you say, and at the crossroads of Europe, how could we have secrets? If there is an answer, it is our preparedness. Every able-bodied male in the country starts National Service at the age of twenty. After four months' training, he goes home but is eligible for active duty until he is thirty-two years of age. Until the age of fifty, he remains on the reserve and attends periodic training sessions."

"But you are such a small country," insisted the Japanese lady. "You could not resist an invasion. Why spend all that money?"

"Switzerland has less than half the population of Tokyo yet we can mobilize six hundred thousand men in forty-eight hours, ready to fight," said Wengen proudly. "The entire population of the country can be accommodated in deep underground shelters. You must have seen some of them—they are visible from many of the major roads. They are also effective against nuclear radiation," he said, adding slyly, "should any of our neighbors be so ill advised as to explode such devices. The most probable answer to Mr. Thompson's question, however, is that any would-be invaders did not consider the effort of conquering Switzerland worthwhile. The country has no natural resources, no coal, no oil, no seaports—"

Across the table a Frenchman, who had told us that he was planning to add a restaurant to his delicatessen in Paris, entered the verbal fray. "Surely it has one natural resource—its strategic location. It is right in the center of Europe."

"But why invade and occupy it?" argued Karl Wengen. "World War Two was perhaps the only time when invasion seemed like a real possibility. Certainly it is the occasion that is uppermost in our minds as it is recent. Did the Germans invade then? No, in the first place, the Alpine terrain would have meant the commitment of large numbers of troops and the possibility of heavy losses. Only men specially trained in such difficult conditions can survive. In the second place, although victory for the German army might be considered to be the inevitable outcome, what would they have gained? No, my friends, it was much easier to conduct their campaigns in Europe and leave Switzerland alone."

"Operate around it, you mean," said the Japanese lady.

"Exactly. There was never a risk that Switzerland would be a problem to Germany while Switzerland remained neutral—"

"With a dominantly German-speaking population, Switzerland would not have had the least thought of acting against Germany in any way," cut in Brad Thompson.

"Precisely," agreed Wengen, "and to look at it from the German point of view, if they had invaded and conquered Switzerland, they would have created for themselves another enemy."

It was a good opportunity for me to put in my contribution. "That makes a lot of sense. Look at Switzerland's neighbors— Italy, already Germany's principal ally; Austria, already part of the Third Reich, German speaking and with a big part of the population sympathetic to Germany anyway; and France, occupied by German forces. This meant that Switzerland was effectively surrounded by countries under German control. Switzerland couldn't possibly be a threat to Germany in any way, and it could have some use as a conduit to the West."

Perhaps that diminished the Swiss position, but if so, Karl Wengen showed no signs of annoyance. "It does not seem to be widely known, but at the end of 1939, we came into possession of some German army training manuals. These treated Switzerland as part of Germany. All the maps included in the manuals did not show Switzerland at all but showed the territory as incorporated into the Third Reich."

"Wow!" said Brad Thompson, "that must have had a bombshell effect on the Swiss government!"

"It united the country in a way that perhaps nothing else could have," Karl Wengen said. "Statesmen, historians, journalists, and military men combined to mobilize the moral resistance of the Swiss people. Interest in Swiss history was revived, and native literature received a huge boost. Romansch, the fourth language of the country and in danger of becoming obsolete, was made one of the four national languages by popular ballot. A great National Exhibition was organized in Zurich and was a big success, despite the times. It was a testimony to the spirit of the Swiss people."

The conversation continued with a spirited discussion of the concept of the Reduit, the theory of fortification that employs one fort inside another in a series of concentric circles. Withdrawal from each territory to the next smaller one continues, and as Karl Wengen pointed out, the willingness to face such sacrifices in land and people was a clear message to a would-be invader.

Breakfast had long since been consumed. The Frenchman who had spoken before said, "More banks than dentists. Isn't that what they say about Switzerland?"

"I have heard that," admitted Wengen with a polite smile. "I think it shows what good teeth the Swiss have."

Most of the other oft-repeated sideswipes at the Swiss came out now that the Alpine ice had been broken. Why had the Swiss refused the vote to women for so long? was the first. Why isn't English taught in Swiss schools? was another. Then came the point that the Swiss men in the army reserve keep their weapons in their homes at all times. Why doesn't this cause an increase in gun crime? We debated until the time for the morning session was approaching.

Helmut Helberg came over from an adjoining table. "You remember we talked the other day about improving the supermarket image?"

"Giving customers more information on foods so that they would buy more of them? Yes, I remember."

"Well, it gave me an idea. Why not make videos of Leighton Vance cooking and show them in the markets? Around the video screen in the market would be racks of the foods he was cooking."

"Sounds good. Have you talked to him about it?"

"I had an even better idea. Have Mallory and Leighton together, husband and wife cooking. Don't you think that would be great?"

"Terrific," I agreed. "Have you talked to him about it?"

Helmut gave me a rueful grimace. "I tried. He cut me off before I was finished. He was strongly opposed to the idea, would not even consider it. Did not want to discuss it."

"Strange," I said. "Maybe you should try him again. You might have caught him at a bad time."

Helmut shook his head. "I do not think so. He is not an easy man to reason with."

I was puzzling over this as we left when Bradley Thompson fell into step beside me. "This is a healthy and wholesome country sure enough," he grunted, "but I'll bet it could get troublesome if it was encouraged."

I walked over to the lobby afterward. As one of the larger lounges adjoined it, the area was a popular meeting place. As I entered, I noticed a young woman at the registration desk. It seemed an unusual time to check in, I thought.

She was short and trim, energetic in her movements. Her hair was cut short and if allowed to grow, was probably a light corn color. She was probably in her late thirties and dressed in a two-piece travel suit. She had only one piece of luggage, I noticed, and it was a small case. She either traveled light or had left at short notice.

Just as I was about to turn away and go about my business. I heard a name that caused me to stop and edge closer to hear more.

The name was "Kathleen Evans."

I tried to gather the context. The woman had apparently asked a question using Kathleen Evans's name, and the receptionist was still shaking her head as part of her answer. The receptionist was not Monique but a different girl. I listened closely, but the rest was just check-in routine.

I watched a bellboy take the woman away in the direction of the chalets, then I approached the receptionist quickly before she could touch the registration computer keyboard.

"You have a message for me, I believe," I said, trying to sound urgent.

The girl turned to look at the racks behind her, and I quickly nudged the screen so that I could read the name just entered. Janet Hargrave, it said, and I had just enough time to swivel the screen back into position before the girl returned with the bad news that I had no message. I showed surprise and looked appropriately saddened.

I had a sudden idea. I had a little time before the morning session began. I knew there was a library although I had not yet visited it. I headed over there now.

It was a large room, dark paneled and a little gloomy as if the spa accepted that guests would be spending far more time elsewhere. I had recalled reading in the brochure that it was strongly oriented toward food and cooking. There stood a long rack of magazines in several languages, and it was not surprising that most were in English. I sought out *Good Food*, the magazine that published Kathleen Evans's column. Inside the front cover of the latest issue was Kathleen's name. I scanned through the names of senior editors, food editors, test-kitchen directors, photo editors, art directors, production coordinators—marveling at how many people it took to put a magazine together. It was almost as impressive as the list of credits that scrolls down the screen at a movie theater and takes almost as long as the movie itself.

 I found her. Janet Hargrave. She was the executive editor of *Good Food* magazine.

CHAPTER FOURTEEN

Leighton Vance was the lead for the morning's culinary entertainment.

"This demonstration is by the special request of a number of people," he began. "The soufflé is by far the most feared dish in the kitchen. There is a popular belief that only a chef can make a perfect soufflé, but that is quite wrong. If you follow some simple steps, anyone can do it."

The room was full once more, and everyone was paying rapt attention. "The oven has been preheated to four hundred degrees Fahrenheit. These ramekins have been buttered twice and coated with sugar. This is one of the secrets—it ensures that the soufflé mixture will rise without sticking to the sides. I'm now taking some butter and mixing in flour in this pan. This is the roux. Continuing to whisk, I am adding a little milk. I am doing this until the mixture is thick." When he had the consistency right, he poured it into a bowl.

"We'll let that cool, and meanwhile I'm taking egg yolks and whisking with a little vanilla flavoring, some oil, and now I'm whisking in the roux and . . ." He poured in a generous amount of Grand Marnier.

"In this electric mixer bowl, I'm putting in egg whites. This is a critical part but not one to be afraid of. The whites must hold a firm peak. One trick that chefs use is to do this in a copper bowl—it stabilizes the temperature. Be careful not to overbeat, or you will see the whites begin to separate." He held out the bowl. He poured in sugar, a little at a time and again beat to stiff peaks. He whisked about a quarter of this into the yolk mixture, then gently folded in the remainder.

"If there are secrets to the soufflé, this folding is one of them. Use a rubber spatula only and keep a rolling motion like this."

He spooned the batter into the ramekins. "Be sure to fill almost to the top. Put the ramekins in a large baking pan of water. Bake for twenty minutes. Disregard those who tell you that drafts don't matter. They do. Resist the temptation and don't open the oven door until the baking is finished."

When the oven door had closed, he said, "There'll be enough for everyone to taste, but in the meantime I'm sure you have questions."

First, though, a round of applause rang out for such a concise and practical demonstration. It had been a fine combination of explanation, encouragement, and some chef's tips. Between questions, Leighton reminded us that a soufflé is somewhere between a party piece, a confection, and a savory. The soufflé is extremely versatile. It can be made with cheese, fish, chicken, eggplant, lobster, shrimp, game, or fruits such as pears, lemons, strawberries, and cherries.

Comments, arguments, and questions were still flying when the soufflés came out of the oven. "The soufflé should be browned . . ." Leighton held out the pan, and there were nods and murmurs of approval of the color. "It should be puffed and set around the edges but still wobbly in the middle." He shook the pan very gently and the audience applauded as if it were amateur hour for hula dancers. As the ramekins were passed around, the room grew rapidly quieter. Applause was universal, and Leighton basked in it.

I made my way to the dining room early. Very early; no one else was there for lunch yet, not even the staff as the tables were already set. I examined the diagram of table settings, then carefully made a couple of changes.

As a result, when Janet Hargrave arrived at the table and took her place, she found herself sitting next to me. I smiled pleasantly, but before I could speak she said accusingly, "You're not Carver Armitage!"

"I am not," I agreed, and explained who I was.

She appeared perplexed. "But you look like him," she insisted. I had to think about that. Hair roughly the same color, approximately the same build and weight, about the same height . . .

"You may be right," I admitted. "We do look somewhat alike. I'd never even thought of that. Still, I'm not him." I explained why I was here in his place.

"Hospital? Operation?" For a moment I thought she was going to start a medical debate and I wondered why.

"Do you know Carver?" I asked.

"We have met," she said briefly.

Before she could take me down any more sidetracks, I took the initiative.

"I know you're Janet Hargrave," I said. "It says so on the seating plan."

"Looks like it's been changed." She was one of those perceptive women.

"They have to make changes when new guests arrive—unexpectedly," I added, and waited for her to contradict that.

She didn't and thus confirmed what I was already suspecting—that she had decided on this trip at short notice. Which gave me the opportunity to say, "One of your star writers was here."

She did not ask who, and it became clear why when she said, "I understand that Kathleen has left."

"Oh?" I said, playing innocent. "Gone back to write up her experiences at the spa? The conference is still on. I thought she had booked for the full week."

Our table was filling up now, and Janet busied herself with introductions—it no doubt gave her an excuse to ignore my comments. When we were resettled and all consulting menus, she asked casually, "You knew Kathleen?"

"I have read her column a number of times, but I had never met her until this occasion."

"Did she think you were Carver Armitage too?"

"When we first met, Kathleen told me I was not Carver Armitage. She was right."

"You mean, she thought at first that you were," she said, her tone of voice suggesting that the fact made her own inquisition of me on that subject perfectly understandable.

"She had some problems accepting that Carver was in hospital too," I said, moving on.

She nodded as if to agree how easy that was. "Which leads me to wonder why it's such a big deal," I went on pleasantly. "Carver was scheduled to come here, couldn't, and I replaced him." I thought it to be an admirably succinct summary, but she did not pursue the issue.

Instead, she said, "You talked to Kathleen, I take it?" She meant it to sound like a casual comment, but she was not the casual statement type. She gave the impression that she was more used to telling art editors she didn't like their art and photo editors how poor their photos were, and complaining that production editors didn't produce.

"Oh, yes," I said with a little emphasis and let the words dangle there. She waited for me to go on, but I chose the moment to place my order for an asparagus flan. She looked at me expectantly when the maître d' had moved on, and I smiled back.

She was clearly figuring out how to ask me what Kathleen and I had talked about, but any tact she might have possessed had been eroded by years of executive editing. "Did she tell you she was leaving?" she asked finally.

I was caught in a dilemma. If I told her about my suspicions that Kathleen had been killed and her body removed, Janet would want to know why I hadn't informed the police. If I didn't tell her, I would be obstructing any efforts to determine the truth. I did the normal, human thing. I compromised.

"We had a date in the Seaweed Forest. She was there, but when I looked for her she was gone. Next morning, I was told she had checked out."

"Seaweed Forest?"

I explained. She said nothing but was snappy at the maître d' when he came around to her side and she hadn't made a decision. He was an expert at herding clients in the direction of a choice and she ordered *soupe au pistou* with mussels.

"She left word where she was going?" she asked.

"Paris apparently, but that's a hub for scores of destinations. Look, you're her editor. Doesn't she keep you informed?"

She played with a fork. "You know who I am?"

"Of course. Nearly everyone in the food business does." It was time to replace the vinegar with a little honey, I thought.

She didn't beam with pleasure, but the compliment slowed

her down. When she continued the conversation, her tone was less belligerent. "It's very important I find her."

"A hot new assignment?" I probed.

She pursed her lips. "I can't discuss our publishing policies."

I took that as a no. "Well," I said, "wherever she was going when she left here, she's arrived by now. She's probably back in the office, pounding the keyboard."

She didn't reply, but I had a strong suspicion that she knew that Kathleen was not back in the office. So where was she and why the mystery?

I had a chilly feeling that she was dead. If so, what was Janet's part in all this? She couldn't know of Kathleen's death . . . could she? Or was Janet here for some other reason?

I ate my asparagus flan and followed with salmon cakes, Szechuan style with a mild curry sauce. Fish was brain food, and if my brain ever needed stimulation, it was now. In fact, it needed a good hard kick in the left lobe.

CHAPTER FIFTEEN

I strolled in the direction of the lake by way of some gentle exercise after the meal. The wooden structure that formed the entrance to the Glacier Caverns basked orange in the dying sun. I recalled the glacier on the Jungfrau with massive chambers as big as auditoriums deep inside its Pleistocene interior. I encountered Axel Vorstahl, who had the same intention of exercise. His fair hair ruffled slightly in the breeze, and his good-humored face broke into a smile.

"I've been looking for the opportunity to talk to you," I told him. "I spent many of my earlier years on cruise ships as a chef. I understand you act as a consultant to the Scandinavian cruise lines."

"That's right," he said happily, "as well as running my restaurant in Copenhagen."

"Cruises must have changed a lot since my day."

"The food on cruise ships has changed more than anything else," he said. "The big Norwegian ships still have their dining rooms with assigned seating, just like the spa here. The ships cater to two thousand passengers or more, but now they offer another choice."

"Competition?"

"The ships now have cafés that operate on a first-come, first-served basis. They are casual and quick and offer salads, soups, sandwiches, pasta, and other light meals."

"The introduction since my day of vegetarian and calorie-conscious meals is another innovation," I said.

"There are other innovations too. Informality has been introduced in lots of ways. Poolside grills, bistro bars where snack meals are served. Many ships now have a resident dietitian. Then too, some lines now offer gastronomic cruises. Guest chefs from famous restaurants are sometimes on board, and the dishes from their restaurants become the highlights of the menu." He laughed. "Oh, yes, my friend, things have changed!"

We talked for quite a while. He was a friendly fellow and we discovered a few mutual acquaintances. "This is my first visit to a spa," I told him. "You have been to others, I'm sure."

"Yes," he agreed. "Quite a number."

"How does this compare?"

He darted me a quick look. "*Ja,*" he muttered, "yes, compare . . ." He seemed to make up his mind. "The food here is very good, very good indeed. But uneven—you know what I mean?"

"Not consistent? The quality varies?"

"Yes, that is it."

"It's been of very high quality since I've been here," I said. "All the meals—and I've been keeping an eye on what others have been eating. It has all seemed to be excellent."

"That is true," he said eagerly. "This time, it has been very good."

"But other times, not so good?"

"Three months ago, I was here," he confided. "The wild salmon was lacking in texture; it was dull, flat, uninteresting."

"Every chef has an occasional bad day," I reminded him.

"The next day, the *veloute de tomate* was underseasoned. It has only garlic in it, as cooked—I am sure you know this—so that seasoning has to be added just before serving. The chef had not done this."

"He is very busy in there while the meals are in final preparation before being served." Why was I making excuses for him? I wondered.

"Busy he may be," said the Swedish chef. "There are many things to do, *ja*. But they must be done. Otherwise the meal is not perfect."

"How often are meals perfect?"

"Not often—but the chef must do all he can to try for perfect. There is no excuse for not seasoning the soup."

"You'd be tough to work for, Axel."

He shook his head firmly. "I don't think so. I demand a lot, sure. But I am fair—and I don't ask anyone in my kitchen to work harder than me."

"I'm sure of that," I told him. "I'll have to try one of your cruise ships."

Until this moment, I had only my own experiences of the food at the spa on which to base any judgment. Axel's wider experience was now suggesting that it varied in quality. A further viewpoint on Leighton Vance's cooking would be interesting. When I left Axel Vorstahl, I looked for Michel Leblanc but could not see him in any of the obvious places. I was near the spa kitchens so I thought, why not give another look?

As I approached, I could hear raised voices from inside. Some sous-chef getting hauled over the coals for not beating the eggs enough maybe. Then a door slammed, and the great khan of the kitchen himself came stalking out. He didn't look to be in an approachable mood, so I didn't approach him. He was storming straight ahead and didn't see me, so I waited till he was out of sight and then entered.

Cleaning up after lunch was well under way and a pastry chef was already rolling out sheets of dough for the evening desserts. Mallory was there, and when I walked over to her a couple of tears were trickling down her cheeks. She quickly rubbed her eyes. "Pepper," she explained with a rueful little smile.

She was putting bones, skin, and trimmings of fish into a large saucepan. She poured in white wine and some water, then a bouquet garni and some salt. She set it over low heat. "A fumet," she explained. "It will be used for a sauce tonight. There will be a *mousseline de poisson*, and the fumet will be the base of the sauce." She seemed glad to have someone to talk to, so I pointed to the three impressive pieces of meat on the bench by her side. "It looks like you're serving leg of lamb too."

"Yes. We have several haute cuisine dishes, but Leighton likes to include one or two that are more country style as balance."

I looked at the bowls of freshly chopped carrots, onions, and celery, the jar of Provençal herbs, and the basket of spinach flanked by a bottle of Madeira wine. "So you're going to prepare leg of lamb à la bourgeoise. I guess it's too soon to take the cream out of the refrigerator. Are you going to bone the lamb?"

"No. Oh, we do when we serve it in the elegant style, but for this peasant way, we don't."

"A lot of peasants wish they ate this well," I told her.

She was cleaning up as she worked, making sure that all traces of fish were removed, as it has a very pervasive odor. I was looking around the kitchen, but I knew I was not likely to see any telltale signs that would confirm or deny Axel Vorstahl's criticisms.

It might have been because she thought that I was going to ask her questions that she didn't want to answer, but I had the distinct impression that she spoke only to head me off. "We're cooking some German and Austrian dishes tonight," she said brightly.

"*Halve hahn?*" I asked. Translated literally, it means "half a hen," but it is a popular local dish in the region of Cologne, and when you order it you get a snack consisting of a hard roll, a slice of cheese, butter, and a glass of beer.

"Oh, we can do better than that," she smiled.

We discussed German cooking. "In many spas," Mallory said, "German cooking is kept to a minimum as it has the reputation of being heavy and fattening. Here, as you have found, we do not make a fetish of diet. Several German dishes are very popular, so we cook them. We avoid most of the ingredients that are high in calories or fats or cholesterol but without affecting the taste."

"Many Swiss enjoy German cooking, don't they?"

"Certainly, Switzerland consists mostly of people of German origin and with German names and habits. Naturally, they enjoy German food, and all the traditional favorites are cooked in homes and in restaurants."

She was surprisingly knowledgeable, and we talked about German cooking for some time. When she began to get that nervous glance in the direction of the door that meant she was afraid that Leighton might return and find her talking to me, I said, "I'd better go. Your husband doesn't like you chatting with the guests, does he?"

"He doesn't like people in his kitchen," she said.

"Lots of secrets to guard?"

"It is a very competitive trade," she said defensively. "He's not paranoid about it, he just likes to think of this kitchen as his private domain."

"He wants to make sure he keeps up his high standards," I suggested.

"Yes. He is very guarded with respect to his reputation."

I wondered what Axel Vorstahl would respond to that, then took my leave, telling her I was looking forward to making a German selection that night.

"Fast food has a bad name," Brad Thompson declared. "I want to change that. There's nothing wrong with food just because it doesn't take three hours to bake. Fast food can be good food—it just doesn't take as long to bring it to the point where you can't wait to put it into your mouth."

It was the afternoon session, and again there was a packed house. How many were pro and how many con remained to be seen.

"Do I need to define 'fast food'?" Brad looked around his audience. His good-natured face and easy manner got him off to a good start. "I will anyway—the fast foods that we know best are hamburgers, hot dogs, and pizzas. Hamburgers and hot dogs are of German origin, and pizza is, of course, Italian.

"But lots of other countries have fast foods. In England they have fish and chips and Cornish pasties; in Belgium, they have fries—or 'frites.' We call them French fries, which makes the Belgians mad because they thought of them first. In the Middle East they have pita and kebabs; in Spain they have their tapas; Indonesia has satays, and Mexico has tacos and burritos."

He was about to continue but a raised hand stopped him. "What about fried chicken?"

Brad nodded amiably. "A good question. We think of the gentleman from Kentucky immediately, don't we? Colonel Sanders."

The same questioner asked, "Was his business really based on a secret recipe?"

"Colonel Sanders himself once said that the seasoning of the batter coating was the secret but added that it did not contain any unusual ingredients. He said that 'the herbs and spices stand on everybody's shelf.'

"That caused a lot of controversy," Brad continued, "between the franchisees and the Kentucky Fried Chicken management. Ray Kroc, the founder of McDonald's—often believed to have secrets of their own in the fast-food market—said that Kentucky Fried's licensees had to pay four or five times the price of the seasonings simply because they were obliged to buy from them."

"Somebody must know," argued another. "Surely the Colonel obtained a patent?"

"He did," said Brad, fielding balls from all directions. "It was for the process only and did not mention seasoning."

"Hasn't anybody had the batter coating analyzed?" came another question.

"Yes. It revealed only four constituents—to the surprise of all concerned. They were flour, MSG, salt, and pepper."

"No exotic spices?" said a disappointed voice.

"Nothing else at all."

A temporary hush settled. Everyone had wanted a secret to be revealed.

Brad resumed his theme. "Young children, teenagers, and adults all love fast foods. The tempo of life today is geared to foods that don't take long to prepare or to eat. We are a lot less formal than we used to be. Sitting at a table with seven or eight knives, forks, and spoons, wondering which to use and going through five or six courses—no, that's not the way we want to eat as we enter the twenty-first century."

As Brad continued, more questions arose. Oriana Frascati was in the audience for this session, and she apparently felt it was her duty to her Italian background to say, "The pizza should get more credit as the ideal fast food. Tell us about its many virtues."

There were laughs at this, but Brad was equal to the occasion.

"It's hard to beat as a fast food, I agree. Okay, the basic pizza was known as 'marinara'—or 'sailor style'—and it was so called because it was one of the staple foods on board the ships of the Neapolitan navy. Those were the days when Naples ruled the Mediterranean. The pizza marinara was made from only four ingredients: tomato, olive oil, garlic, and oregano—"

"No cheese?" asked an incredulous voice.

"Cheese wouldn't keep on a long voyage," explained Brad. I was pleased to learn that he had an interest in the history of the pizza and went further than merely knowing how to bake one. "In the city of Naples—still considered the birthplace of pizza—cheese was used, and it was mozarella, made from buffalo milk. Other areas of Italy developed their own variations. In Rome they used onions instead of tomatoes; in Liguria, they used both."

The school principal whom I had encountered before spoke up. She seemed to be at least as interested in food as in education. "For us cooking dummies, it would be more helpful if you told us about the dough. Isn't that more critical? Seems to me anybody can put what they want on it after that, and it'll cook in the same time it takes the dough to bake."

"Makes sense," nodded Brad. "Originally, flour, water, and yeast formed the dough. Yeast had already been developed centuries earlier for beer making, so although many other kinds of yeast are available to us today, it was beer yeast that was first used for pizza dough."

"Today," the principal called out in the tone she must have found highly effective in her job. "How do we make pizza dough today?"

"There are lots of ways—"

"Tell us one," came the insistent interruption. "The best one."

Brad was doing a masterly job of not losing his cool. "Sure. Mix whole wheat flour, a little salt, and a little bicarbonate of soda. Make a well in the center and put in some yogurt, water, and olive oil. Mix into a dough and knead it on a floured board." He paused and his silence said, "How's that for brevity and simplicity?"

Inevitably, further questions took him into the realms of variables, but he had done a fine job of sticking with the essentials, and he got a big round of applause when he concluded.

I made my way to one of the public phones and dialed the number I had noted from the issue of *Good Food* magazine. I was offered several numerical options by the electronic operator, but I opted for the 'stay on the line' contact and got a real live person. She had a pleasant female voice.

"I want to speak to Kathleen Evans," I said.

"Who's calling please?"

"It's Thomas Mann," I said, giving the first name that came into my head. He had written about a spa and it was in either Germany or German-speaking Switzerland.

"I'm sorry, Mr. Mann, she isn't here," the operator said. "Can someone else help you?"

"I really need to speak to her. I have some information she is waiting for, so if she has told you she doesn't want to be disturbed, I can assure you that she would want to be. She is very anxious to hear this."

"I understand, but she is not here—truly she isn't."

"She's in the office somewhere, though, isn't she? I know she was at that conference in Switzerland, but she's back now. She told me she was leaving the conference early."

"Well, she's not back here yet," she said hesitantly.

"You're sure of that?"

"Yes. I tried her at home too and she wasn't there."

As I paused to think, she asked, "Can someone else help you?"

"Yes," I said, "put me through to Janet Hargrave."

"I'm sorry, she's not here either."

"Can you tell me where I can reach her?"

"I'm—er, not sure—"

"She's there, though, isn't she?"

"No, she isn't." The girl was beginning to wilt a little between her excessive use of negatives and steering an uncertain path between loyalty and lying.

"She said something about going to Switzerland too," I said. "She can't have left already?"

"She left yesterday."

"Yesterday? That was sudden, wasn't it?"

She saw a way to put an end to all these questions and took it.

"Yes, it was sudden. It surprised us all."

I thanked her and hung up. So Kathleen hadn't been seen since . . . well, since I saw her in the Seaweed Forest. As for the story about flying back—if that were true, she had not been to her office or her home. So where was she? I had a chilly feeling about that all over again.

Janet Hargrave knew more than she was telling me, that was plain. Of course, there was no reason she should confide in me. Still, she had evidently flown here for some reason connected with Kathleen, and it sounded as though it had been a hasty decision on Janet's part.

If Janet was looking for Kathleen, she really wanted to find her—flying to Switzerland at short notice betrayed unmistakable urgency. What could Janet learn here? I wondered. Whatever it was, she would have a hard time finding it, or so I was guessing. That meant that she might clutch at any straw, ready to accept any help she could get.

Even from me . . .

CHAPTER SIXTEEN

The Swiss are not cocktail drinkers. As most of the guests at the spa were not Swiss, that factor did not necessarily apply so perhaps there *was* something about the Alpine air that turned the taste buds in another direction, away from alcohol. The fact remained that cocktail drinking before dinner was not a heavily attended function.

I remarked on this to Gunther Probst, who was the other one in the lounge. He was drinking Scotch on the rocks, and I was having a vodka gimlet—I only drink when I'm on a job.

A "job" meaning an investigation. . . . Well, this hadn't started out that way, but if it wasn't an investigation now, it was a darn close facsimile.

"South Germans prefer a spritzer before a meal," he commented.

"It's a pleasant drink," I conceded. "Hock and seltzer water. The extra kick in a cocktail that comes from a higher alcohol content, though—it is refreshing."

"It helps the mental processes, I always say."

"In need of some stimulation, are you?"

He held up his glass and looked through the amber liquid pensively. "This isn't going to be as easy as I thought."

"Putting food recipes on disks?"

"People are doing that already, I know. I planned on going a couple of stages further."

"Leighton Vance can help you there," I said. I display a touch of adolescent malice when provoked, and I hadn't liked the way Mallory had wiped away tears when I had almost interrupted a scene of domestic conflict in the kitchen. If I could divert Vance into other areas of activity, he would have less time to cause distress to Mallory. I resolutely ignored the voice that was whispering, "None of your business."

But Probst shook his head. "He can't."

"Can't—or won't?"

"Says he's too busy."

"He does have a very busy kitchen to run. This place is full right now. You can see his point of view." I was trying to be reasonable.

"The best people to help you are those who are the busiest."

"Maybe it says that on page three of some millionaire industrialist's best-selling memoir," I said. "I've had a lot of help from busy people myself, but I get a rejection once in a while. A high-quality kitchen is a place where you can expect such a rejection—there's an awful lot to think about and keep track of."

"I suppose," Probst admitted. "I guess I just like to be rejected a little more graciously."

"Ah," I said, "grace! Now that's another matter."

We both laughed and had another drink. Elaine Dunbar came in, wearing light gray slacks and a gray jacket of light wool with a silky weave in it.

"Haven't seen you in these last sessions," I told her.

She ordered a Campari and soda. "I've attended a couple," she said. "Must have been different ones."

"Could be," I agreed. "Hope you're finding them more rewarding than Gunther here."

She raised an eyebrow, and Gunther repeated his problem.

"Our chef's uncooperative, is he?" she said. "I'm going to be approaching him in the very near future. Maybe I'll get more out of him." She sounded as if she relished the prospect of a reluctant witness.

Brad Thompson came in then and asked for a double martini. He was followed closely by Oriana Frascati, who wanted only a glass of mineral water. The conversation fragmented from that point on, and we went into dinner.

Bearing in mind Mallory Vance's promise of German dishes, I scanned the menu. Sure enough, Leighton was offering several. *Konigsberger klopse* was there and so was *wiener rostbraten*. The latter is a dish I often cook myself at home. It was Cole Porter's favorite, and it is one of mine too. It is simple, in fact deceptively so, and requires close timing. In addition, Leighton was offering *kalbfleischvogeln,* veal birds with the unexpected anchovies; *rehrucken,* loin of venison; and *spaetzle,* Germany's answer to pasta. I chose the *wiener rostbraten,* always hoping that another chef will cook it better and I can find out how. It was not as good as mine but partly redeemed by the Bordeaux that I had with it. This was the Fleur-Cardinale, whose producers are now buying up vineyards in the Napa Valley, where they intend to make an American Bordeaux that is just as good as its French progenitor.

The next morning, Michel Leblanc led the parade with a class in bread baking. Caroline told us in her introduction that this was one of the cooking subjects that had been most requested. It seemed that so many cooks, confident in other areas, felt that their bread was not the superior product they wanted it to be. Good bread was not enough—they wanted to bake great bread. So here was Michel Leblanc to teach us how.

"Most of us don't like the bread we buy," he began. "Steam baked, precut, plastic wrapped—modern bread typifies the mechanical approach, the output of a production line, all the nonhuman approaches to food that we are now finding undesirable and unacceptable."

Murmurs of agreement greeted this opening, and Michel went on. "Untouched by human hands—doesn't that typify bread? Under the guises of hygiene and economy and convenience, we are being fed this inferior product. Now we are rebelling." He thumped a fist on the table and dishes rattled. Anyone sleeping would have had a violent awakening, but no one was. "We have been making bread for eight thousand years, and we want to go back to making it properly." Someone clapped.

"Bread is basically a simple food. I am going to show you how to make the simplest version of all." He waved to the ingredients in front of me and began, describing each action. "Take flour and eggs, more whites than yolks. Add yeast until the mixture thickens, add sugar and let it rest." He pulled a doughy mound toward him. "This has been prepared in exactly that way and baked. Now I cut off the crown, pour in some melted butter, mix it well, replace the crown, and bake again."

He slid it into the oven and beamed at his audience.

"That is the way bread was made a thousand years ago, and it is still the basic way. Nothing has really changed, but naturally some improvements have appeared. Beer yeast was the only kind available then, but today refined yeasts are used. Emulsifiers are added to keep the bread from going stale quickly; kneading is done mechanically and is more efficient. Perhaps the most useful improvement has been in the oven. Modern ovens hold a constant temperature—very different from the days of continually stoking a fire, which caused the temperature to go up and down."

A barrage of questions followed, for it seemed that despite the variety of breads on the market, many people got a certain satisfaction from baking their own. Helmut Helberg was in the audience, and I gave another star to Caroline de Witt when Helmut said she had specifically requested his presence. A good-natured altercation between Michel and Helmut developed over home-baked bread versus supermarket bread. Perhaps it was inevitable that Helmut should have the last word by pointing out that his chain of supermarkets carried all the ingredients for the home baker.

We were late disbanding for lunch and most of the attendees at the session headed directly for the dining room, where, as Michel had told them, there were ten different kinds of bread being offered with the meal.

I took a brief promenade by the lake to do some thinking. Janet Hargrave was the person who had me baffled. She was executive editor of a magazine, and one of her columnists who had come here to the conference had disappeared. Janet had come here to . . . to do what? Find her? Unusual behavior for an editor surely.

If I had been a real investigator, I would have observed Janet going in to dinner and taken my trusty lock pick to her cabin. Inside, I would have prowled through her belongings. It wouldn't take long, I thought, as she had arrived with only one small bag. I would have found unmistakable evidence that . . . Well, that was the way it was supposed to work. I wondered if it ever did. People's motives were not usually so simple that a single piece of paper explained them fully. A photograph, that was another popular giveaway; yet if photographs were that incriminating, why did people carry them around?

For a real investigator, it sounded as if all the conventional approaches would be a waste of time. It was a good thing I was merely a Gourmet Detective—it meant I could be unconventional. So what could I do? Well, I could talk to Janet Hargrave and get her to confide in me. Was I being unrealistic? Well, I had one big factor in my favor—I knew more about Kathleen's most recent activities than Janet did. I would have to use that.

The lull in the period before lunch was a suitable time to catch someone, and Janet proved easy to waylay. I had noted her cabin number when she had checked in, and I hung around in sight of it until she came out and headed for the dining room. I fell into step beside her.

"I think we should have a chat," I told her, putting on my disarming smile.

She gave me a sour look. "What about?"

"About Kathleen Evans."

She almost broke her stride, but that was her only reaction. Still, it was better than being ignored. We walked on, and at length she said predictably, "What about her?"

"I didn't tell you the whole truth before." I had decided that throwing myself on her mercy might pry something out of her.

"I thought not."

"What do you mean?" I asked, startled.

"You said you had a date with her and she was there but

when you looked for her, she was gone. That sounded like a cover-up."

"You took me by surprise, showing up like that."

"Go on," she said in a neutral tone.

"It was true that she invited me to meet her in the Seaweed Forest."

"I took a look at it early this morning."

"Good, then you'll have a better appreciation of what I'm telling you." I went on to relate what had happened. By the time I finished, we had stopped walking and she was facing me.

"So you don't know for sure that she was dead."

"No," I admitted. "She looked to be, but I didn't have the chance to feel for a pulse. Then she was gone. She might have recovered, got out of the Seaweed Forest, and hidden out until she could take a cab to the airport."

"And the alternative?"

"That's where it gets really speculative. If she was killed, why did someone take her body?"

She eyed me shrewdly. "You don't ask the obvious question—why should anyone kill her?"

"I don't know the answer to that. I'm telling you all this because I think maybe you do."

She turned half away. "She's a columnist on a food magazine, for Christ's sake. Why would anyone want to kill her?"

"Her column's in your magazine—you tell me."

From the distant lake, voices were raised and drifted across the water. She looked that way, then said, "She's a food columnist, not a secret agent."

"If you think she's dead, that's not an answer."

"We may find that she's back in New York, at her desk and writing up a story on the spa."

"I don't think so," I said flatly. I didn't elaborate and she said nothing. She had probably called the magazine herself already.

"Do you have anything else to tell me?" she asked coldly.

"No, but I hoped you'd have something to tell me."

She was starting to shake her head, but I think my attitude told her I was going to press for some kind of an answer. "I can tell you this," she said. "Kathleen has been here to the spa before."

"On business?"

"Yes."

"Does that mean something?"

"If so, I don't know what it is," she replied.

We both waited for the other to make a further contribution but neither of us did. At least she had told me something, though I thought she was still holding back. It would be understandable if she thought I hadn't told all. My story sounded fishy even to me.

"We may as well go to lunch," she said, starting to walk briskly toward the dining room.

"We must do this again," I suggested. "Maybe a few more meetings like this and we'll know enough to really find Kathleen."

CHAPTER SEVENTEEN

Who was the busiest busybody at the spa this week? Who would be the best storage house of gossip? I needed a fink and I decided it must be feminine. I acknowledged that that might well be a typically male sexist point of view, but, to me, the female of the species is the most efficient conduit for picking up tittle-tattle, rumor, hearsay, and scuttlebutt.

Which female? Millicent Manners came to mind at once as the least abstruse of those present, and she was a good place to start. I recalled her saying that she did an hour of aerobics each morning before breakfast, and with the superbly equipped gym here, that was where she would be.

She was there, under a monstrous machine that she was heaving into the air with arms and legs. Other equipment surrounded her, all of it looking complicated and muscle jarring. Dials and panels showed how much effort she was expending and how many more agonizing moments of this torture remained. Millicent was not quite alone in her dedication to physical fitness, but almost. An elderly man was struggling with some ropes that he appeared to be trying to pull out of the wall, and a woman nearly his age was pedaling a bicycle that was not moving an inch. Otherwise, the gym was empty.

I waited until Millicent stopped for a rest. I didn't want to interrupt her, as from the effort she was expending it looked as if the machine might fall on her when she ceased pushing. It didn't, though, and she crawled out, reached for a towel, and headed for the water cooler to replenish her body fluids.

She was still breathing hard and I wanted her in top tittle-tattle shape, so I waited a little longer. She hadn't noticed me, and when she finished her third cup she turned abruptly and went into the shower and changing rooms. That was even better. When she came out, she would be full of self-righteous health and energy.

She did have a glow, I had to admit, and I told her so as we walked out of the gym together. "I haven't seen you in there before," she said.

"I like to keep a low profile when I exercise," I told her.

"You didn't even raise a sweat," she said with a twitch of her lips.

"I have a high threshold," I told her. "We don't have many exercisers, do we? Or maybe people like to come in later in the day. Kathleen Evans was telling me she liked to exercise before dinner."

"Kathleen Evans?" she frowned. "Oh, the food columnist. I haven't talked to her."

It was not an encouraging start. Maybe she was too wrapped up in herself and her career, I thought, but as I quested further I found that she was a brighter woman than I had at first believed. She told me of the changes she had proposed in the scripts and of the studio's willingness to go along with her on them. She had to insist on this week at the spa so that she could get a better understanding of food and cooking, and since the shooting of the first scenes had been delayed, they had agreed.

"Anyway," she added, "I needed a break like this. I've been shooting for fifteen months on *Tell Me You Love Me*."

As for Kathleen Evans, though, when I brought up her

name casually, Millicent had nothing to say. She hadn't talked to her and commented that she hadn't seen her in the last couple of days. As we reached the dining room, I was prepared to drop that line of investigation and find another prospective informant.

Marta Giannini was my next choice. She didn't qualify as your typical, motor-mouthed busybody, but she was friendly and talkative, happy to chat with everyone. She was gregarious and lively; she got around and might have spotted signs or observed liaisons that a mere male would miss. Besides, I liked talking to her, though to do so I had to dawdle over my breakfast of fresh fruit, muesli, and coffee, as she was evidently sleeping late this morning.

When she finally came in, I waved and she joined me. "Just coffee," she ordered. "Nothing else." Feeling some hunger pangs after her second cup, she managed to devour a couple of pear Danish, which the Swiss call Viennese, and then she had a slice of pumpernickel toast with blackberry jam. She looked refreshed and sparkling, and though she wore little makeup in the mornings, I noticed that she never neglected her eyes, which she rightfully considered her outstanding feature.

"I need a walk after that." She sighed, adding that now that she had more or less retired from acting, she could afford to indulge in a few occasional carbohydrates. On the lawn, we stopped to watch an impromptu volleyball game, which, as it was being played without a net or lines, was causing much good-natured argument about the score. Marta was clapping her hands and crying out in delight like a schoolgirl at every outstanding play.

"You're a sports enthusiast," I said. "I should have known from that movie where you trained your pet horse to run and then won the Kentucky Derby with it."

"I was terrified of that horse. It was so *big*. I kept asking for a smaller one."

"So now you've gone from horse racing to volleyball."

"Oh, is that what this is?" she asked, wide-eyed.

"In a way. I think I saw that food columnist playing it the other day. Come to think of it, I haven't seen her around since that day, have you?"

"Kathleen Evans? No, I heard she'd gone back to the States." She tossed out the comment, then groaned as the ball flew wide of what would have been the court.

This was a promising start. Marta was more alert to the movements of the present inhabitants of the spa than I had expected. "I heard that too," I said, "that was why I asked. I thought she was supposed to be here for the whole week."

"I thought she was too." Marta's enthusiasm for sport was waning before my eyes as she was finding a good gossip more exciting. "Perhaps she found a good story for her column here at the spa."

"Surely not," I said, trying to keep her going. "Not here at the spa?"

Marta pouted. "Are we so dull?"

"Kathleen writes a food column. It's not society or film scandal."

"The two might be combined."

I flashed a glance at the profile that a couple of decades ago had appeared on film posters throughout the world. Her eyes were on the volleyball game but her thoughts weren't.

"Come on, Marta, you know some juicy tidbit, I can tell."

She laughed, a short throaty laugh that had at one time devastated me. It still had an effect even if it was a little diluted by time.

"I used to say to Hedda, 'You tell me a story and I'll tell you one.' "

"And did she?"

"Oh, yes. Hedda would do anything for a story, and swapping them satisfied us both."

"Your stories were always about you?" I asked.

"Most of them."

"Were they true?"

She shrugged. "Once in a while."

"So your story on the spa—is it about you?"

"No."

"Is it true?"

"Yes," she said coyly. Few sophisticated women can be coy, but when they have appeared in fifty or so films, I suppose they have learned coyness along with all the other feigned emotions.

"So you're not in this story," I said. "That's disappointing. I was picturing the scenario . . . I see you in a dirndl and a bonnet, running across an Alpine meadow, arms outstretched, and toward you comes a baron in lederhosen. In the background, I hear the sound of—"

"No, it's not that one," she said with an amused smile. "They already made it—mind you, I would have been much better in the part than Julie. But that's okay, she is one of my friends now, so I won't criticize her performance. No, there's no music in this one—but I'll make up for that and give you two stories."

"Twice as good. Carry on."

"I said they are not about me—they're about Kathleen Evans." She paused for dramatic effect, and there had been a time when no one in Hollywood could outdramatize Marta.

When she thought a long enough pause had elapsed, she said quietly, "Kathleen likes chefs."

I nodded. "Probably collecting background material." I said it dismissively and it worked.

"In the sauna?"

"Ah, that could be seen in a different perspective," I conceded. "Still, journalists have to get their material wherever they can."

She snorted. It was elegantly done, but it was still a snort.

"Which chef was she with?" I asked, trying to sound only semi-interested.

"I don't mention names," she said haughtily, but then she reverted to coy. "This chef, though, well, he had probably left his poor dear wife cleaning up in the kitchen."

Leighton Vance. Well, that was not a complete surprise. "You said two stories. You also said 'chefs' so a chef is in the other story too?"

"Oh, good shot!" Marta called out, her eyes back on the game, but I knew it was only to provoke me as the ball had hit someone on the head and rocketed into the air. I looked at her until she turned to smile at me. "The other? Well, there aren't that many chefs here, are there? What about you, for instance?"

For a fleeting moment, I thought she was referring to my assignation with Kathleen in the Seaweed Forest, but I confined my stuttering and stammering to the inside of my head.

"I'm not a chef anymore," I said.

"What are you?" she wanted to know, and her tone was more serious.

I told her. I told her that I was called "the Gourmet Detective" and I explained what I did. I told her about Carver

Armitage and how he had talked to me from his hospital bed and asked me to come to the spa to replace him.

"So you're a detective," Marta said pensively. She brightened. "I was in one of the *Pink Panther* films!"

"Wasn't it the one where Colin Gordon was the murderer?"

"Oh, I don't know. I never could follow those plots. Do you carry a gun?"

"Certainly not, and like I keep saying, I'm not really a detective." I went through it again, stressing foods and spices, cooking methods, my love of the history of foods and avoiding all mention of corpses and crime, mystery and murder, deceit and death.

"You're sure you're not on a case?" she asked, her expression showing doubt.

"The only reason I came here to the spa is to substitute for Carver Armitage. That's the truth." It was—as far as it went. This was not the time to consider sins of omission versus commission, and anyway the mysterious happenings had occurred after my arrival here.

She nodded in satisfaction. I felt ashamed of myself for misleading her and mentally promised that I would make amends—but not just now.

"So it's all right for me to tell you about the other chef?" she asked.

"Go ahead."

"I want you to know that I am not a scandalmonger—"

"I never thought you were. Tell me and stop teasing, Marta."

She crinkled her eyes in a smile. It showed up the lines,

but that didn't matter. "I saw Kathleen talking to Michel Le-blanc—twice."

"Surely that's not—"

"Once was in the Roman baths. They were in a very se-rious conversation. Another time was on the lawn. They were well away from everyone else, and Michel seemed to be shouting and waving a finger at her."

Michel. Now that *was* a surprise. The mild-mannered Frenchman seemed much miscast in that role.

"I hope it helps," Marta said.

"What do you mean?"

"In your investigation," she said, turning her unseeing gaze back on the volleyball game.

"I told you I—"

"I know you did. If I can help any more, just ask me." She tired of volleyball and began to walk away, but she tossed a final comment over her shoulder.

"I love mysteries, even if I can't understand them."

CHAPTER EIGHTEEN

I was on duty once more at ten o'clock in the morning. Again, I was obliged to follow the schedule set out by Carver Armitage, as the various presentations had been planned so that a wide range of foods and cooking styles could be covered without duplication. Carver had selected roast duck with orange as this morning's dish.

The conference room, modified with portable equipment, was full, and I noticed Elaine Dunbar in the second row. Tim Reynolds was there, this time with a different lady, a statuesque redhead. Marta was there and so was Helmut Helberg. Karl Wengen was present, Gunther Probst came in, and Millicent Manners entered at the last minute. The indefatigable Caroline de Witt introduced me.

"This is one of the most famous dishes in the world," I began, "and it can be eaten in a different version in every country. It's a national dish in France, where they claim that the Rouen and the Nantais ducks are the best due to the crossing of domestic ducks with wild drake. Florentines point out that the duck is included in their cookbooks of the fifteenth century. In England, the Aylesbury duck is considered the best, whereas in the USA, the canvasback duck is popular but the Long Island duckling reigns supreme. It has a distinguished heritage, for in the nineteenth century one of the first Yankee Clippers brought nine Peking ducks from China. Millions of Long Island ducks are descended from that stock."

On the bench in front of me was a fine bird. "This is a duck with Nantes ancestry, although it is from Alsace. It weighs four and a half pounds. Heavier than that, a duck begins to get tough." I pulled the bird toward me and took a long, sharp knife. "First, I'm cutting off the head and the feet . . . now I'm plucking the feathers. I'm removing the wishbone, greasing inside with butter, sprinkling with salt, and pricking the skin so that some of the fat can escape."

I put the bird into a roasting pan—"the smallest possible," I advised. "Meanwhile, some butter has melted in this pan. I'm adding some sugar and pouring it over the bird. The oven is preheated to three hundred and fifty, and I'm putting the dish in. Some prefer to braise on top of the stove. Either way, it will take one and a half to two hours."

I indicated the makings of the orange sauce: the peel boiled in a small amount of water, the juice with a little Curaçao, several slices, a few spoonfuls of bitter orange marmalade, some tarragon vinegar, roux, and chicken stock.

"The efficient staff prepared a similar bird and put it in the oven an hour and a half ago," I said, "so let's see how it is." It was nicely browned, and I removed it while I added some meat stock, some flour, and some sherry to the juices in the pan. I heated for a few minutes, stirring constantly. I put the bird back in the pan and added the orange sauce, heated quickly, and put the bird on a large heated plate. I cut the duck into quarters, poured the sauce over them, and spread the slices of orange on top.

"I'll cut these up so you can all have a taste," I said. "The

French insist that potatoes do not go with duck, but in England and Germany at least, roast potatoes are served with it. Peas, carrots, turnips, and glazed onions go very well."

While everyone was tasting, I mentioned the other ways of cooking duck: Bordelaise style, in which the duck is stuffed and served with cèpes—small mushrooms; casserole style; in a curry; braised with olives; with sauerkraut; with cherries; with apricots; with applesauce; and in a terrine, a pâté, or a mousse.

"Some chefs prefer not to stuff duck at all because it give off too much fat and the stuffing will absorb this. The roasting temperature can be higher, but today's more fat-conscious cooking suggests a slow and gradual melting of the fat so that it can be siphoned off with a baster.

"The kitchen here prepared an excellent terrine of duck," I added. "Some of you probably had it. Anyway," I went on, "the versatility of the duck is obvious from these few examples in which so many fruits and vegetables go well with it."

The duck that had been passed around was gone in minutes, and several people proclaimed their intention to wait until the next one was ready for consumption too. Questions flowed. "What about Oriental ways of cooking duck?" was the first.

"My favorite among those is Bali style—the duck is stuffed with spiced cassava leaves. Most Indonesian restaurants serve it."

"How do you know when to stuff a duck?" was another question.

"If you want to use stuffing, then it should be a duck. With duckling you may or may not, as you choose," I answered.

"Is there any reason to braise rather than roast?" was the next question.

"The best rule to follow," I said, "is to roast a wild duck but to braise a domesticated duck."

"You can see why my problem gets worse," said Gunther Probst mournfully as the session broke up. "So many foods, even just the ones to go with duck."

"It makes you all the more useful," I argued. "Manual recording is not nearly as efficient as your method with the computer. You can handle so much more data."

"I guess so." He sighed.

No one had left. Everyone was still there, discussing and asking more questions. Helmut Helberg came across the room. "I should sell more duck then, should I?"

"It has a lot going for it," I said. "It's low in calories and has no cholesterol. Most cooking methods bring the fat way down. Ducks are easy to raise, so they are potentially cheap."

"They make a good alternative to chicken and turkey," he agreed. "I'll have to look into that." He nodded in satisfaction. "Lobsters the other day, duck today—yes, I am getting a lot of ideas here."

A lady with her hair tied back and wearing an expensive-looking suit came to tell me how much she enjoyed the presentation. "But what about duck soup?" she asked. "You didn't mention that."

"It was the title of a very funny Marx brothers film," I told her. "It's not a soup at all. You can, of course, put pieces of cooked duck into a soup just as you can so many of the foods found in the kitchen."

People finally began to filter out, and Elaine Dunbar was one of the few left. "I don't eat duck very often," she said. "Maybe I should try it more; sounds like it comes in lots of ways."

"I think you'd enjoy it," I told her. "In fact, I'll have a word in the kitchen—maybe they can put another duck dish on the menu."

"I'll have it if they do," she said.

"Meanwhile, are you thinking up more ways of linking cooking with crime?"

"Seems to be no problem. The Coca-Cola trials and appeals ran for more than ten years, did you know that?"

"I didn't realize it was that long. Contrasting drinks, though, on that basis, the legal wrangles over the right to call a beverage 'champagne' ought to run for a century!"

"They well might. It goes over great in the media too," Elaine said. She was becoming animated. "Here's this tiny area of France, the department known as 'Champagne' fighting the rest of the world, claiming that if a sparkling wine is not made in Champagne, then it isn't champagne. The public loves the David versus Goliath contest."

"The problem with champagne," I suggested, "is how to distinguish the different brands from one another. By taste? No, it's by image, the taste is irrelevant."

"Surely lots of connoisseurs can tell the difference. Isn't that what wine tasters do?"

I was about to answer when she said, "Look, I was just going to go to the baths. Why don't you join me? We can continue this debate there."

I didn't reply immediately.

"Something wrong with that idea?"

"Ah, no. I've had a couple of experiences there that I wouldn't want to repeat."

She looked at me curiously. "Not in the baths, surely?"

"No, not there—"

"Right," she said promptly. She was a young woman who usually had her own way, that was obvious. "See you in fifteen minutes."

A winding path led into the cavern baths, where the steady drip and gurgle of condensing and flowing waters echoed from the rock walls. Inside, it was like a vast subterranean palace with two large marble pools interconnected to form a figure eight. Shining green ferns in red clay pots glistened damply, and black wrought-iron and wooden beach-style chairs and chaise longues were strewn around the edge of the pools.

Bronze dolphins spouted water into the pools, and a gentle mist rose from the water surfaces. Hidden lighting in the ceiling of the cavern threw a green cast on to the scene below. It all looked like a set for *Indiana Jones Finds Atlantis.*

A slight murmur rose and fell. It was not from the denizens of the spa gasping with pleasure in these hedonistic surroundings but evidently from the cycling of the equipment, feeding, filtering, and exhausting the water, which had a blue-green tinge. This was mostly due to the green lighting because the pools were not lined on the walls and the bottoms with the conventional aquamarine tiles but consisted instead of sheets of reflective glass.

No one was here, to my surprise. I walked past the edge of the pool, where I had to pry open a heavy door of foggy glass to see beyond it. It was a sauna room filled with scented steam that flooded out to engulf me. At first, I could see nothing, then very slowly I realized that there was a row of slatted wooden seats all around the walls. One end of the room was much hotter, and the steam became a denser white.

Only one person was there. She was female, naked, and sat propped against the wall in an awkward position, eyes closed.

CHAPTER NINETEEN

My immediate reaction was, "Oh, no, not again!" but as I plunged through the steam, her eyes opened and she smiled.

"Must have fallen asleep," Elaine said. "What took you so long?"

My look of alarm puzzled her. "What's the matter? Haven't you ever seen a naked woman before?"

It must be pleasing to always have the right thing to say on the tip of one's tongue. Maybe those who do have a repertoire from which they can pick the appropriate bon mot, but only a very extensive repertoire would contain a snappy response to Elaine's question.

Luckily, she was not disposed to silences, either her own or those of others, and she went on, "Your clothes are getting wet. Better take them off." I must have hesitated because she said, "It's all right. There's no one else here."

"What was it we were talking about?" she asked eventually, her voice as foggy as the air in the sauna.

"Wet clothes?"

"No, before that."

"Champagne, wasn't it?"

"Yes, that was it. We finished that conversation, didn't we?"

"I think so," I said as there came noises from the pool area: a couple of loud splashes and then voices that echoed metallically from the cavern walls.

"Let's start another conversation out there," Elaine said.

Outside the sauna room, pristine white terrycloth robes hung on a rack, and we put them on. In the pool, two shapes were thrashing through the water and another two swimsuited figures sat by the water's edge.

We took a couple of wrought-iron chairs well away from them. "We went very quickly from Coca-Cola to champagne," I said, "but I'm sure there are lots of other potential cases that you have your eye on for your legal future."

"Endless."

"Is your fiancé in the legal profession too?"

"I don't have one," she said carelessly, watching the two stroking, splashing swimmers.

"I thought you said—"

"I did. I often say that as a smokescreen. Keeps unwelcome attention away."

The other two figures, one male, one female, dived into the water, and the scene was like one from an ambitious art film with the mirrored walls and bottom of the pool having their images chopped into slices by the churning water.

"I didn't realize you were a detective when we first met." Elaine's tone was conversational.

"But now you've realized it?"

"Somebody told me, I don't remember who."

"I'm not really a detective," I said. "I often have to explain this. I hunt for rare foods, seek out obscure herbs and spices, advise on food substitutes and sources, unusual cooking methods.

I help out wherever a knowledge of the history of food is concerned. Someone nicknamed me 'the Gourmet Detective' and it has stuck."

She listened with interest. "A fascinating job," she commented.

"Some of the time. Like other jobs, there are stretches of routine too. Of course, you could have found out all this by just asking me."

She leaned back in the chair and smiled. "I rather like this way better, don't you?"

I returned her smile.

"You never get involved with any Sam Spade stuff then?"

She was watching the swimmers again, so it was hard to guess if there was anything behind the question.

"Very rarely."

"Most of your clients aren't in the restaurant business, I take it?"

"Some of them are, certainly," I said.

"No crimes in the kitchen?"

"Sorry, counselor," I said, "but can you make your line of questioning more specific?"

"Very well, Your Honor. Have you ever run across murder in a restaurant? It must be an easy place to commit such a crime. After all, many foods can be poisonous, or can contain poisonous substances—or so I understand."

"That's specific," I admitted. "All right, I was involved in a case not too long ago where a murder was committed at a banquet. Poison was involved in that one. As to a murder by poison in a restaurant—no, I can't say I've ever run across a case like that."

She nodded slowly, very slowly, and I waited for some

exposition but none was forthcoming. "Are you going to tell me more?" I asked.

She pursed her lips. "Mmm, no, I don't think so."

"You can't ask a question like that and then just drop the subject," I protested.

"I'll have to drop it if you can't contribute," she said tartly.

"I can't contribute, but surely you can—this is your story. What restaurant? Where? When?"

"You missed 'who' and 'why.' " She smiled as she said it. She had a nice smile when it came from her human persona as opposed to the professional, the lawyer. "I don't know the answers to most of those queries, and I'm only guessing at the others."

Another couple came in and joined the swimmers in the pool. Voices and water noises became tangled with the echoes from the rock walls and roof. "This is the case you mentioned before, isn't it?" I said. "You said that the case was being reopened."

"Yes, this is the one."

"It has a fascination for you, doesn't it?"

"Yes."

"Well, whenever you want to tell me more, maybe I can become fascinated too."

She nodded. "Lawyers often hire private investigators, you know."

"I told you I'm not a—"

"You told me, yes."

She regarded me with that look clever teachers give to backward pupils sometimes. It means "I am wiser than you. I know more about this than you do." She turned her gaze on the swimmers for a moment and when she looked back at me, it was an appraisal, an assessment of how I might fit into her plans.

For my part, I was wondering if I should tell her about Kathleen Evans and her mysterious death—or disappearance—or both. Maybe I should, I thought, but not now. Kathleen's fate had nothing to do with Elaine's case, and after all, Elaine was a lawyer, about to launch a career. Unless there was a client, she had no reason to be involved.

Come to think of it, I had no reason to be investigating Kathleen and the circumstances surrounding her sudden disappearance. I didn't have a client either, although I had been involved during her last day—if that's what it was.

It was disappointing. This encounter with Elaine sounded now as if it had been planned for the purpose of ensnaring me in—well, I had no idea in what. The invitation from Kathleen Evans to meet her in the Seaweed Forest now shone in a new light. Maybe Kathleen had had the same motive—to involve me in some plot or at least find out what I knew. I would have preferred to think that it was me they wanted, but it was looking as if that was erroneously self-centered.

We walked back to the main buildings. "Just in time for lunch," she reminded me. It was hard to comprehend that it was that early in the day, as so much had happened. Still, it's nice to know that a woman has a healthy appetite.

Although there was no formal seating arrangement for the midday meal, I didn't see Elaine when I entered. I took a seat next to Tim Reynolds, who promptly began a conversation. "Just the man I'm looking for—well, one of them anyway. It's my wife's cousin. Ex-wife really—second ex-wife, that is. Stan's a good friend; we go to football games together. He wants to open a restaurant and he's looking to me to invest in it. Called me last night. Can't do it without me, he says. Now, I've been careful with my money, but it's dwindling nevertheless. If I put money in Stan's restaurant and it failed, I'd be in bad shape. What do you think? Is it a good investment?"

I told him of the main factors to consider, starting with location. I asked about Stan's history and the discussion went on through my fennel stuffed with feta and Kalamata olives followed by haddock in rice paper with a shallot, red pepper, and soy sauce. At the end of it. I had to tell him that it sounded chancy. He sounded disappointed, and I told him by all means to get further opinions. On the other side of me, the Japanese lady was anxious to ask me what I thought about her nephew's future if he persisted in wanting to marry high technology to the fishing industry. I was cautiously optimistic, and she nodded in satisfaction, though it might have been at her grilled mahimahi with green tomatoes rather than my advice.

After the meal, I saw Elaine. She was deep in conversation with two men and seemed to be doing most of the talking. I was leaving the table when Janet approached me. "Have a good meal?" I asked her.

"What? Oh, yes, it was fine." She didn't sound inclined to describe it any further than that and stepped aside from the others leaving the table but stood facing me.

"Can we have a chat? There are some points we need to discuss." She was brusque, and tension showed in her voice.

"Certainly," I said. "I have a session at two-thirty and I need to run over Carver's notes first. Can we talk afterward?"

"All right. I'll attend the session. Which conference room are you in?"

"Six A."

She hurried out and I stared after her, wondering what was behind this request.

CHAPTER TWENTY

The afternoon session was by special request. A number of guests had said that they had specific questions, and Caroline and her team thought the answers might be of interest to all. Consequently, a panel was put together consisting of Michel Leblanc, Leighton Vance, and myself, with Caroline de Witt as the chairperson. At least I supposed that was what she was, though I was judging by her manner and bearing, which were certainly autocratic even if I had no way of classifying her as unduly feminist.

"Tell us about stir-frying," invited a woman with a Scandinavian accent. "It's not a cooking technique that most of us grew up with, not having been born in the Orient. Cookbooks don't help—they just say 'stir-fry.' "

Caroline looked at the panel for an answer. Leighton Vance looked airily at Michel, who answered. "A Chinese wok is a very good investment. A heavy frying pan will do, but a wok is certainly the best. It was designed exactly for the job, which is a very rapid transfer of heat."

Vance didn't seem inclined to continue so I went on, "Stir-frying has the advantage of being fast, as Michel says. Its disadvantage is that the preparation time is longer because all the ingredients need to be chopped finely. Frozen vegetables, by the way, can be used frozen, they just take a few seconds longer. The order of stir-frying the ingredients is important. The vegetables should always be cooked first. The sauce should be added next. Some recipes don't call for one but I always like to use one, as vegetables are dry without a little liquid.

"The basic sauce consists of chicken or vegetable broth with cornstarch or flour to thicken and a little soy sauce. It is important to remove this before introducing the meat, chicken, or shellfish, otherwise there is a tendency to overcook."

Michel added, "Stir-frying is very simple and it is preferable to use a wok or a pan that you can hold comfortably in one hand so that you can use wrist action to stir with the other hand."

"What are sweetbreads?" Tim Reynolds asked. "I've always wanted to know."

There came a few sympathetic laughs, no doubt from others who didn't know either.

Leighton Vance was ready with the answer for this one. "It's the thymus gland of a lamb, calf, or young steer. When animals grow more than a year old, their thymus gland shrinks and disappears."

"What's a thymus gland?" Tim persisted. Someone laughed, and Tom turned and shrugged. "I'm not a chef, that's why I asked the first question. I'm not a doctor either."

Michel stepped in at this point. "It's a small gland in the neck. It helps make white blood cells."

"I never did see a good reason to eat it," Tim called out.

"They have to be eaten immediately, as they are extremely perishable," said Michel. "Sweetbreads are a good source of protein, but, sadly, they are very high in cholesterol."

Caroline looked over the room and selected another raised hand. "What exactly are 'andouilettes'?" was the question. "We see them on menus in French restaurants and here in Switzerland too, but we're not quite sure what they are."

Leighton looked disdainful, as if he felt that anyone attending these classes should know the answer, so I answered.

"They're called 'chitterlings' in English. Pigs' intestines. They are seasoned and then shaped like sausages. They are poached, cooled, and then grilled. Lyonnaise and Strasbourg styles are the most popular."

A string of other questions followed. One interesting one was, "Is it all right to drink a cocktail before dinner? It doesn't spoil the taste of the food?"

"Certainly not," I said promptly. "A good cocktail puts you in the mood for a good meal and stimulates the appetite. My only rule is not to drink gin before having a meal with red wine."

"I drink only wine," Michel said. "Perhaps being brought up in a region full of vineyards is the reason rather than any matter of choice. I have tasted martinis and don't like them."

Leighton Vance declined an answer, and no one pressed him.

"Is it acceptable to use frozen foods?" someone asked.

Leighton came to life on this one. "You will find no frozen foods in our kitchen, nor do we microwave," he said firmly.

Michel Leblanc disagreed. "Some frozen products are very good—you have to be selective, of course."

"As many of us cook at home," I added, "it's reasonable to keep a supply of frozen foods there."

I hadn't noticed Helmut Helberg, but he spoke up now from a seat near the back. "The sale of frozen foods in our markets continues to increase. Convenience is a big motive for many people, and this segment of the market must be catered to—but besides this, frozen foods can be kept a long time. They are high in nutrients and not harmed by storage."

Other questions referred to specific dishes and how to cook them, but before they could be answered, Caroline rapped on the table. "We have had numerous requests of this type," she said, "and here's what we are going to do. The day after tomorrow, we will give demonstrations of cooking as many of these dishes as we can. These will run throughout the day. A schedule will be posted so that you can pick the time that a certain dish will be demonstrated." She consulted her notes. "So far, we have cheesecake, fondue, cassoulet, and if there are any more requests, please let me have them right away."

As we began to break up, Caroline came over to us before we could leave the podium. "Which dishes would you like to cook?" she asked with a smile, looking from one to the other.

"Leighton should take fondue, as it's a Swiss dish," I suggested. He nodded, without enthusiasm but with no objection either.

Michel smiled placidly. "Cassoulet must be my fate, surely?" he acknowledged.

"Inevitable," I told him. "I'll do the cheesecake."

"Good," said Caroline, the perfect organizer. "If each of you gentlemen will let me have your list of required ingredients, we will see that they are all waiting for you."

I had noticed Janet, but though she had been attentive, she had not said a word. We moved on a converging course as we approached the door. As we walked along the corridor back in the direction of the lounges, one of the blond staff girls came out of a doorway and was walking near us. Janet looked straight ahead stiffly.

When the girl turned off, Janet said quickly to me in a low voice, "I'll meet you in the herb garden in ten minutes." I had time only to nod and she was gone, walking on past me.

I had been intending to visit the herb garden, but this was the first time that the opportunity seemed to have occurred. I had asked an herbalist once, "What is an herb?" and she had replied, "An herb is a plant that makes you feel better and become healthier." Some of the herb garden was outdoors, neat squares of leafy green plants with pods and seeds and flowers of numerous hues.

A much larger area was a minijungle—or so it appeared at first glance. Closer acquaintance showed it to be well tended and lush, with herb- and spice-bearing bushes. Some of these rose waist high but would recede with the season. Splashes of blue and purple accentuated the deep green of the foliage and splotches of red and yellow made it as good to look at as it undoubtedly was for the health. I could see rue, coriander, annato, cumin, and vivid yellow patches of saffron. I knew that Saffron Guilds still existed in all the major Swiss cities, and the national crop continues to increase.

I could see no sign of Janet, but the large greenhouse where the more delicate herbs were being raised was probably where I would find her. She had worn a definitely clandestine air when I had left her after the session and was no doubt keeping out of sight.

The greenhouse was a large building, as big as an aircraft hangar. The big glass panes were scrupulously clean—although I would expect no less in Switzerland. They were misted, though, enough to obscure vision and I could see only blurry green vegetation inside. I went in—in to a humid, fetid atmosphere. The temperature was clearly controlled and then I realized that the humidity was probably at a high level, as many of the plants in here would be from tropical climes. Still, it seemed hot and sticky after the cool, clean Alpine air outside.

Plants in boxes and barrels filled the place, while around the glass walls, shelves held trays of seedlings. The atmosphere was a jumble of aromas—so many that none stood out. It was rich and sumptuous, heady and almost overpowering. People obviously didn't stay in here very long.

Right now, no one had stayed, it seemed. I could not see people or hear voices. Janet was in here somewhere, though, and I set out to look for her. Moving was like forcing a path through thick aromatic smoke, and I was aware of perspiration prickling out all over my body. I called out, but the dense air choked the sound. I came to a turn near the glass wall and the first objects I saw were two bare legs.

They stuck out from a spiky green bush. I pushed the stems aside. Janet was there, eyes closed, and I could not tell whether she was breathing. She was wearing short khaki shorts and a white halter. I was trying to lift her to a sitting position when I noticed a hissing noise. At the same time, I became aware of a sweetish, cloying smell, certainly not that of a plant or herb.

The atmosphere was getting thicker by the second. It was impeding my breathing, and I was having to take big gasps to get more air. I hadn't taken many gasps when I knew that this was a mistake. The hissing noise was the release of some kind of insecticide spray, and at the speed with which the greenhouse was being filled, the spray was soon going to be equally lethal for humans. I tried to hold my breath as I pulled Janet's body out of the undergrowth and in the direction of the door.

I was drenched in perspiration by now. It dripped off my face as I bent over her body, desperately dragging her along the floor. She seemed unbelievably heavy, I thought. My progress was too slow, and I would never make it to the door.

CHAPTER TWENTY-ONE

One more turn and I would reach the door. . . .

Almost there—with nearly my last gasp I grabbed the knob and twisted. Nothing happened. Frantically, I twisted, turned, pulled, pushed—even kicked—but without result. Again and again I tried, unwilling to believe that the door would not open. Finally, out of breath and desperately tired, I collapsed on to the floor beside the inert body of Janet.

At ground level, there was miraculously a little more air. Evidently the sprinklers were on the ceiling, and the chemical spray took a little time to settle. I gulped in a life-giving lungful of air, let it rejuvenate my blood, exhaled, then inhaled again as deeply as I could. It gave me a brief respite, and I had to make the most of it. I battled with the door again. Still without success.

Furious and angry, I kicked at the nearest glass panel—then let out a yelp as pain stabbed through my ankle. The glass remained unbroken. I dropped to the floor, positioned myself as carefully as impatience and fear would allow, aimed both feet at the panel and lunged with all my body weight. Pain jabbed through both ankles—it was either unbreakable glass or an extremely tough plastic.

I heard a moan of anguish. It was a strange sound and it took a few seconds to realize that it was coming from me. I collapsed on to the floor again, this time awkwardly. I found myself turned away from the door and through the fog of insecticide, still thickening insidiously, I saw a partition with various dim shapes near it.

I crawled a few yards closer so that I could make out the shapes. They were various pieces of equipment, evidently used in maintaining the grounds. The nearest of them was a lawn mower.

It was the type with a big engine and a seat. I felt a surge of hope. Somehow, I found a tiny reservoir of energy to crawl nearer and pull myself on to the saddle of the machine. Surely it was too much to expect that the key was in the ignition?

It was too much to expect. The key was not there, but my eye fell on the partition wall. A panel mounted there had what looked like dark clusters on it. Could they be keys? They were, and I fumbled for the nearest bunch.

The greenhouse was growing darker, and I knew I was close to losing consciousness. The keys did not fit, and I threw them aside. Another key hanging by itself looked to be the right size, and with panic closing in, I knew I was almost out of time.

The key slid into the lock and I twisted it furiously. To my indescribable relief, the engine fired at once. The machine was parked facing out of the storage area and I rammed a foot down where the accelerator should be. The mower leaped forward like a spurred racehorse. Barrels crashed, boxes burst, and stands crunched as we lurched across the greenhouse, bouncing and skidding. I caught a glimpse of light coming in through glass panels, and I wrenched the steering wheel, heading straight for it.

I went through the transparent wall in a cascading shower of glass shards. The wave of fresh air hit me like immersion in icy water, and I almost passed out. Then my vision began to clear, and I breathed deeply to get the contaminated air out of my lungs. I was bouncing over a grassy slope. The release from the choking confines of the greenhouse was intoxicating. The mower raced on faster and faster.

My mechanized steed went roaring down the slope, which was getting steeper by the second. Too late, I remembered that my foot was still flat on the accelerator. A silvery gray mass ahead of me was spreading like a huge stain. It spread faster, filling my vision.

It was the lake, and I was too close to do anything but plunge into it.

The cool Alpine water was a wonderful stimulant. My head went under and something hard bumped against my knee. It was no doubt the magnificent machine that had saved my life. I had not had time to take a breath, and I was gasping for air as I broke free of the surface and saw that I was only yards from the edge. A few strokes was all it took, and I was wading in mud and then onto the springy grass.

I struggled up the slope. I had thought that the air and the water had revived me, but I found that the fumes had taken their toll. I was utterly weary but I couldn't stop, for Janet was still in that deadly greenhouse. I battled my way uphill.

It wasn't that far. The nightmare conditions of my desperate escape and the suffocating effect of the fumes had made it seem much farther. I reached the hole in the wall of glass. The lawnmower had done a spectacular job, and the hole looked to be four or five times larger than the projectile that had made it.

The atmosphere inside was largely clear already, the fumes seeping out into the evening air. There was still an unpleasant chemical smell, like a mixture of hospital carbolic and rotting vegetation. I kicked aside broken herb containers, pieces of

splintered wood, and shattered shelving, following my way back
to the storage shed where I had found the mower.

From there, it was only a short distance to where Janet lay.
Or should have lain.

She wasn't there.

Perhaps I had miscalculated or my memory was faulty. I searched
all around in a pattern that took me to the glass walls on the
nearer sides. Still nothing. I set out on a search that led me up
and down every aisle in the building. Perhaps she had crawled
away, trying to escape. I realized that now I was assuming she
was still alive, whereas I had thought before that she was dead.

The whole scenario was assuming a definite aura of déjà vu.

To be certain, I covered the greenhouse again. No body.

Had the crash of the glass been heard in the main building
complex? I wondered. No one had shown up to investigate. The
hydrotherapy units were farther away, and the noise had probably not reached that far. I went out through the jagged glass
hole and to the main entrance of the greenhouse. It was still
locked, but there was no key.

It was then that I saw a large sign erected outside the door.

WARNING! ACHTUNG! AVIS! AVVERTIMENTO!
During the next three days, the automatic insecticide spray
treatment will be in effect in this building. Patrons of the
spa should not enter the greenhouse during this period, as
the chemicals used in the insecticide may be harmful to
humans.

The notice was repeated in German, French, and Italian. If they
needed any confirmation of just how nasty the chemical was to

humans, I would be able to provide a testimonial. That might not be a good idea, though. The notice had not been there when I had gone in, and the door had certainly not been locked.

Someone wanted me to have an "accident" . . . but was it me? Maybe it was Janet they were after. She must have come in first. So where was she now? If the attempt had been successful, why had the body been removed?

It was not just déjà vu. There was a precedent for it. Kathleen Evans had been killed in the Seaweed Forest and she had disappeared. It couldn't be coincidence. There was definitely a pattern emerging. First a columnist from *Good Food* magazine and now its editor.

The pattern was getting more and more sinister too. For two bodies to be removed from the spa cast a strong suspicion on the staff. Was Caroline de Witt masterminding some plot, aided by some of the blond staff beauties? A less likely place for such a thing to be happening was hard to imagine. A respectable spa, widely known and with prominent clients? Absurd. . . .

A voice cut through the clear air. I realized that I was standing there, dripping lake water and getting chilled to the bone. The voice was not too close and had no tinge of urgency in it. I waited, then went over to the outdoor herb garden, its colors faintly tinted in the light of a moon that was sliding out from behind the Alpine peaks to the north.

I had a wider vista from here, and in the dim light I could make out three or four figures making their way back to the main buildings. Two or three of them were talking now. They must have come from the hydrotherapy units, and that gave me an idea. I didn't want to go back into the main building area looking like something dragged in from the lake—even if I was. In the hydrotherapy center, several of the buildings had racks of white terrycloth robes. I could take one of those and be less conspicuous.

The lure of water therapy was proving popular. Several people were coming and going and I had to be alert, but I managed to grab a robe, crumple up my sodden clothes into a bundle, and carry them under my arm. As I walked back to the main building, all seemed calm and peaceful. I recalled a previous occasion—I had been looking for Kathleen's body and I had been unable to understand why no alarm had gone out then.

Was this going to be the same?

Pools of orange light lit the approaches to the main buildings of the spa. As I walked toward the nearest building, I encountered Marta Giannini and Axel Vorstahl out for a stroll.

"Aha," Axel said, "getting some water treatment?"

"I think I've had all of that I can stand for today," I said.

I was aware that they were both looking with amusement at the bundle of wet clothes under my arm, dripping water.

"I had another mud bath," Marta said gaily.

"It has made you look radiant," I assured her.

They walked on, and I hastily made my way back to my chalet and temporary security. This place was getting to be dangerous.

CHAPTER TWENTY-TWO

The first thing I did was to call Janet's room. As I had expected, there was no answer. I took a shower and let the hot spray pummel my body. This was too much. Two women, both appearing dead—but were they? Both disappearing? Or had they? Well, Kathleen certainly had disappeared and it would be only a short time before it would be clear if Janet had disappeared also.

They both worked on the same magazine . . . that was the odd coincidence that was probably not a coincidence at all. It must be a key to these bizarre happenings. So why were they happening here?

After breaking out of the greenhouse, I had toyed around with the idea that Caroline de Witt was pursuing some criminal plan, but the more I examined that idea, the more absurd it seemed. What plan could possibly be operating in a spa, especially one as popular as this? It was true that cover-ups would be easier for staff members to arrange, but I could not rule out the possibility that guests were responsible. At least that possibility applied to Kathleen's "disappearance," but now with Janet's "disappearance"—if that was what it turned out to be—some more elaborate explaining by the management was going to be needed.

A big hole in one glass wall of the greenhouse, for example.

The reaction to this suddenly appearing aperture would be a signpost along the road to solving the puzzle.

Drinking time before dinner had been severely eroded, and by the time I emerged from the soothingly hypnotic influence of the hot shower and dressed, it was the dinner hour.

I went through the lobby again as before, taking the temperature. Once again, it was normal. Everyone was going about their business as if nothing had happened. Staff members sauntered or scurried about, attending to their tasks just as they always did. Guests asked at the desk about messages or at the cashier's office about currency or banking transactions. The fax machine was in demand, with missives flying in and out. Phones rang, were answered, and voices filled the air. As to anything out of the ordinary—nothing, absolutely nothing.

Every time the main door opened and someone came in, I expected to see a man in uniform. None appeared. I saw one of the blond staff girls passing through, and after a brief study of her walk, I concluded it was Julia. She came closer, and I confirmed the identification. She smiled as I greeted her.

"Busy as always, I see. Still shorthanded?"

"Oh, yes," she said, "but we all enjoy our work."

"This vandalism hasn't caused you more work, has it?"

She looked puzzled. "Vandalism?"

"There's a rumor that there was a break-in at the greenhouse."

"Oh, that . . . it's just a rumor. One of the gardeners tried to drive a mower out and the controls stuck. He ran into the glass wall."

So that was the party line. I went into the dining room. Oriana Frascati and Michel Leblanc were my immediate companions. "Are you contemplating a Swiss cookbook?" I asked Oriana. She had her hair swept back and looked quite attractive in a severe way. "Or is there one already?" I added.

"In Switzerland, there are several, but a book on Swiss cooking written in English? Nothing recent has been published."

"Is that because there are not considered to be enough Swiss dishes?"

"Probably," she said.

"Swiss chard and Swiss rolls don't count?"

As a spot check on her sense of humor, it worked well enough. She smiled. "After *Geschneltes*, it's hard to find as many as are needed to fill a book. The favorite dishes of the Swiss are all claimed by the French, Germans, and Italians."

The stuffed green olives that had been my choice of the first course arrived, super colossal size, and the stuffing tasted like a mix of sausage and veal. Michel had a stir-fried hot and sour cabbage salad, and Oriana chose a zucchini risotto.

Michel Leblanc leaned across to address Oriana. "It must be getting harder to find new approaches for cookbooks."

"It is. We've even exhausted the noncooking cookbooks."

Michel looked puzzled. His English was excellent but it was easy to understand why that expression baffled him. Oriana smiled as she saw his expression.

"We've been having a flood of them for some time. "The *I Hate to Cook Book, I Can't Boil Water*, and *Fifteen-Minute Meals.*"

Michel smiled and nodded. "Ah, I see. Books for beginners. That is good."

"Then we had the humorous cookbooks," said Oriana. She rattled off a list that included *Nobody Knows the Truffles I've Seen, Gourmet Cooking for Dummies*, and *Desperation Dinners*.

My ploy was working well. Now I was able to turn to Michel Leblanc. "Have you written any cookbooks, Michel?" "No, I have not. Many articles for magazines and newspapers but not any books."

"Magazines? Ah, of course, yes," I said, "I was just trying to remember where I had seen your articles. One was in *Good Food*, wasn't it?"

Michel hadn't mentioned any television appearances, but if he had made any, they hadn't sharpened any latent acting ability. He looked down at his plate, reached for the salt (which he didn't need), and said in an uncertain voice, "No, I haven't, er, been in that magazine."

"You're going to be in a future issue then?" I asked. "Didn't I hear Kathleen Evans say something about working with you on it?"

Mentioning her name seemed to embarrass him. "No, we haven't discussed it."

"So what were you talking about in the Roman baths?" was the next question, but I didn't want to ask it at the dinner table. I compromised with, "She's a good food writer, isn't she?"

He mumbled what might have been a grudging agreement, but it trailed away and Oriana was saying, "We have a book in preparation with favorite recipes of famous chefs. Perhaps we can get you to contribute to that?" Michel grabbed eagerly at this lifeline, and the arrival of the entrée brought a halt to the conversation. I had selected the fritto misto, tiny fillets of lake fish that are found commonly in Swiss lakes—perch, trout, pike—and served with basil mayonnaise on the side. Michel was having a pork stew, which probably had Hungarian origins, and Oriana explained her choice with "I've been hungering for a steak all week. Just a simple one with a green salad."

I was pondering my next ploy when Oriana handed it to me—on a plate. "The food here really is excellent," she commented.

"It is," I agreed. "We must congratulate the chef—yet again." I put down my fork and gave a plausible impression of having been struck with an idea. "In fact, the food is so good that you should talk to Leighton about a cookbook."

"I did," said Oriana, attacking her steak with gusto. "He said no."

"Really?" I was sincerely puzzled. "I would have thought he'd leap at the chance."

"He doesn't even want to contribute a recipe."

Silence didn't exactly fall as the sounds of happy eating continued, but it was an additional fact to add to the complex picture of such a potentially great chef. Was he shy about publicity? He didn't seem to be shy in other regards.

I tried not to let these conundrums spoil my meal. They didn't. The fritto misto was perfect, just crunchy enough but not laden with batter. The basil mayonnaise had been made with a light touch, and as this was a Swiss dish I decided on a Swiss wine and ordered a *vin fletri*. In France, such wines are known as *vins de paille*. The word *paille* means straw, and the wines are so named because the grapes are laid out on beds of straw to dry out. This can increase the sugar content, and the French version is more of an after-dinner wine, but the waiter assured me that the Swiss version is lighter and drier. And so it was.

A slice of what the French call "the embroidered melon" completed the meal. The raised, lighter-colored network on the rind gives this melon its name. It is called a canteloupe in the United States, a situation complicated further by the fact that what Europe calls a canteloupe is not grown commercially in the United States.

After the meal, though, the questions kept coming into my mind. Two women had disappeared. Both might be dead. In my search for clues, a name had come unbidden to the top of the heap—a name that should have occurred to me sooner when I considered who might be able to contribute some meaning . . . Carver Armitage.

I might be doing him an injustice in suspecting him of knowing more than he had told me. Perhaps he had been intending to come to the spa and talk about food. Perhaps he had tried to get others to replace him and couldn't. I recalled that the universal surprise in finding me at the spa was really surprise that Carver Armitage was not there. But perhaps also—just perhaps—there might be more to it than that.

From the public phone, I called St. Giles's Hospital in London. A string of helpful voices bounced me round a circuit before I was talking to Sister Blackstone. She had an ice-encrusted voice and an Arctic manner. She must strike terror into the hearts of the nursing staff, I thought, and her patients must dread the sound of her approaching footsteps. Certainly, Baron Victor Frankenstein would never have selected her as his assistant on that fateful night when thunder clapped and lightning flashed through the dome of the castle laboratory—he would have feared that she would terrify his creation.

"Mr. Armitage?" she repeated. "Yes, he was under my care."

Poor fellow, I thought, he'll never be the same again. I said, "Isn't he still there in the hospital?"

"Of course not. We discharged him some days ago."

"I thought he was going be there another week?" I said.

"Certainly not," she said firmly. "Not for such a minor matter."

Minor to you maybe, I thought, but for Carver a matter of great importance.

"Was his treatment, er, successful?" I asked, trying to keep our line of communication open.

"We considered alternate treatments," she said loftily. "Amputation was one of them but—"

"Amputation!"

I probably groaned.

"It wasn't a serious matter," her flinty tones told me. "He wouldn't have missed it."

She must have heard me gulp. "I don't know him really well," I explained, "but I think he would have considered himself disastrously incapacitated had you used the knife on him."

She sniffed. It is not easy to convey a volume of meaning in a sniff, but she did it admirably. I didn't need to ask in order to know that she did not agree with me.

"So how did you treat him?" I asked.

Her voice hardened, if that were possible. "I must question your authority to ask such questions over the telephone. Just who are you? Are you a doctor?"

"I'm his half brother," I ad-libbed. "I just came back from Zimbabwe."

"Zimbabwe?" she repeated, and skepticism dripped out of the telephone.

"You probably call it Rhodesia—us old hands do most of the time."

"In that case, you should call Mr. Armitage and ask him these questions."

"We've sort of lost touch—you know how it is." There was no answer. Apparently she didn't know. I went on, "Besides, matters of a sensitive nature such as this require delicate handling even between half brothers."

"Sensitive! Delicate! What's sensitive or delicate about a painful end joint, little finger, left hand?"

Was this jaunty hospital jargon? I wondered. Euphemisms of the profession?

"He *was* in the impotence ward, wasn't he?"

The silence that followed could have swallowed an Alp.

"For a little finger?" Her scorn would have daunted the Russian army. "No, he came in for an examination. He left before noon."

"Did his doctor send him?" I asked.

"Of course not. He came in of his own accord."

My mind was spinning. Carver had admitted himself to St. Giles for a miniscule matter that sounded like a hangnail and called me at that time. I had to admit that it was a great way to get sympathy, especially the "male thing," which guarded against probing questions.

"Thank you, Sister," I said weakly, and hung up the phone.

So Carver had wanted me to come here in his place. He had gone to some lengths to make sure that I did so.

Had he wanted me to get killed in his place?

CHAPTER TWENTY-THREE

How do you investigate when there is nowhere to go? No doubt real detectives would know what to do. With vast armies of men and women, inexhaustible files and highly ingenious computers, they find a score of avenues to explore. But a food detective like me . . . I was always explaining to people that I'm not a detective at all, really. Now I had to believe it.

Two missing women and two attempts on my life—maybe three. Must be enough clues there, somewhere. . . . Even the fictional detectives would be able to find them. If Sherlock Holmes were involved, he would be puffing on his pipe. Lord Peter Wimsey would be gazing at one of his rose beds, Nero Wolfe would be seeking inspiration in a bottle of beer, whereas Mike Hammer would be pounding his fists into a face, any face. No help to be found there. I didn't smoke a pipe, didn't own a Ming vase, liked beer but didn't find inspiration in it, and abhorred pugilistics.

Carver Armitage's antics baffled me too. Getting me to feel sorry for him and then dispatching me here where I would be a target for assassination was not friendly behavior. It was true we were not exactly friends, but it was not the behavior to use even with acquaintances.

It was the next morning, and I was feeling frustrated. Breakfast had not helped the mental processes, and I had a couple of hours before the morning session was to start. Plenty of time to find clues—if only I knew how.

"Ask questions" was the only useful piece of advice I could give myself. It lacked brilliance, I admitted. It might be dangerous, I warned myself. Initially, there was only one place to start. I went to the public phone and called Carver's number in London. There was no answer, and his answering machine did not even respond.

I went to the reception desk. Monique was not on duty this time. It was a very young man with slicked-down hair. He had a Swiss-German accent and was trying to grow a mustache with very little sign of success. I used the same ploy as before.

"Is there a message for me?" I gave him my name and when the inevitable head shake came, I frowned in disappointment. "That's strange. I had a breakfast appointment with Janet Hargrave and she didn't show up. I've looked everywhere and can't find her."

He was eager to help. He called her room and got no answer. He pushed keys on the computer, looked surprised, then said, "Just a moment" and went to the cashier's desk. It was a rerun all the way. When he came back, he said apologetically, "I'm sorry, Miss Hargrave checked out."

"How did she go?"

It was the same answer as with Kathleen. "A taxi to the airport."

Behind me, a voice said in an incredulous tone, "Janet Hargrave's left?"

It was Elaine. She was wearing a yellow-and-white shirt and white slacks, looking more appropriately dressed for lunch on the lawn than for the upcoming cooking presentation.

"Yes, she has," I told her.

She looked perplexed. "That's abrupt, isn't it?"

"Very. You've been talking to her?"

"Yes." She looked around. It was not a furtive movement, for she was not a furtive person by any means. Still, she obviously didn't want any eavesdroppers and that made me very curious. She moved away from reception and so did I. She wouldn't be easy to grill, but maybe I could learn something if I employed all the techniques that I recalled from both real and fictional detectives.

"I talked to her too," I said. That was one of my limited repertoire of ruses, and it was intended to make the witness think that you knew more than you really did.

Maybe it was working. She shot me a look of surprise. "What were you talking to her about?"

Ouch. Elaine had a more direct approach than I did.

"She was concerned about Kathleen Evans."

That came close to scoring a hit. If Elaine was going to cross-examine in court, she might want to brush up on non-chalance.

I decided to follow up and show how honest I was being. "Kathleen left very abruptly—like Janet."

"Yes, I know. I talked to Kathleen too."

I recalled seeing the two of them in conversation and thinking that they had looked as if they might already have been acquainted.

"I believe you knew her previously, didn't you?"

"No," she said. An emphatic head shake reinforced the word.

"She seemed to have some other reason for being here and not just doing a story for the magazine," I suggested.

"I wouldn't know," Elaine said. She seemed to consider a more cooperative reaction. "Well, she might have," she conceded. "I wish I was sure what it was."

"Does this have some connection with your murder case?"

"Frankly, I don't see how it can," she said, meeting my eyes. "But there might be some tenuous link."

"What does that mean?"

"Well, for instance, some person connected with my case might be involved with what's going on here at the spa."

"Is something going on here at the spa?" I asked with all my most bright-eyed innocence.

"Shall we take a stroll?" Elaine offered.

We went outside and along the wide concrete walk between the reception and the next building, the one with several conference rooms. Other strollers were out too, especially those who were having guilt pangs after the rich Danish pastries, the heavy pumpernickel bread, the creamy omelettes, and the German sausages. Elaine waited until no one was within earshot.

"You're an investigator," she began. "Kathleen Evans has left suddenly and now Janet Hargrave has too."

"I don't see how you can put those three facts together and come up with any kind of conclusion."

She shook her head. "It's not something I need to prove."

"I am not here for the purpose of investigating. I came to replace Carver Armitage, who is unfortunately hospitalized. What did you find out about Kathleen's abrupt departure?" I asked.

"Well, she isn't back in her office."

"Maybe she has another assignment."

"I don't think so," she said, watching me for telltale reactions. "Her office thought she was still here."

So Elaine had called *Good Food* magazine as well. The girl there must be wondering by now about all these phone calls. She would be wondering even more if Janet didn't return to the office.

I was in a quandary as to how much I should confide in Elaine. Whatever it was she was looking into just might have something to do with the strange happenings here at the spa, although her description of it as being a "tenuous link" suggested that she didn't think so.

"Maybe we should pool information." I tossed it out lightly.

She took it the same way. "Maybe. You first."

"Kathleen asked me to meet her in the Seaweed Forest. She was there but when I, er, wanted to talk to her, she disappeared. She hasn't been seen since as far as I can make out. She has not gone back to her office, and when I asked about her here, they said she had checked out and taken a taxi to the airport."

It was as near to the truth as I wanted to venture. As to whether Kathleen was alive or dead, my best guess was that she was dead, but I wasn't ready to bring that up until I knew where Elaine stood.

"You called her office?"

I had expected her to be astute enough to catch that. "Yes. As you did."

"And now Janet has disappeared just as abruptly," she said, reflectively.

I nodded. "Now it's your turn. You said we'd pool information."

"I said 'maybe.' "

"If you have something to hide, it makes me suspect that you are more involved in this than you're admitting."

We reached the end of the concrete walkway. We stopped and faced one another.

"Give me one more day," she said. "I have some phone calls to make. I expect to learn enough to clarify a lot of points."

I didn't have a lot of choice. Nevertheless, I tried to sound as if I were being magnanimous as I paused and then said, "All right, but one thing—don't call from your room—and Elaine . . ."

"Yes?"

"Be careful."

She looked surprised, as if the thought had not occurred to her that she might be in danger. I did want her to be careful but at the same time, any hint that she was threatened might render her more likely to share information. I ought to be ashamed of myself for using such tactics, I thought. Lord Peter would never do anything so ungallant. No, but Mike Hammer would, came my immediate response.

The morning session was to be a hands-on affair, and well before ten o'clock all hands were on deck and eager to get in on some culinary action. Leighton Vance and Michel Leblanc were joint presenters today, and the subject was puff pastry.

Lines of tables were set up and trays of ingredients were on each one. The "students" sat in rows. Marta Giannini sat at the front, looking glamorous in a new cooking outfit that must have come from Emmanuel Ungaro rather than Williams-Sonoma. Oriana Frascati was looking studious and already had her notebook open and was gazing at a screen full of moving stars. Helmut Helberg was carefully tying a large apron around his substantial middle, and I heard Millicent Manners saying, "I am really looking forward to this—it's just what I need to learn."

"The greatest discovery of the modern kitchen," was Leighton's opening statement. "That's what Auguste Kettner called puff pastry," he went on, "and the emphasis is on 'the kitchen' because that is exactly where pastry originated. Other culinary discoveries have come about in other ways, but pastry comes from the kitchen."

Michel took up the presentation at that point. "The most difficult pastry of all is the puff pastry, so we are going to teach you how to make this. When you have mastered puff pastry, all the others come easy. In French, we call it *mille feuilles*, and you will see why in a moment. This is the kind of pastry used in *vol-au-vents*—I like to translate that as 'gone with the wind,' which describes how light it is."

"I'm going to describe what Michel is doing," said Leighton. "He has flour on the pastry slab and is adding salt. He is making a well in the middle of it and is pouring water into it. Now, he is mixing it into a smooth paste. He is leaving it to cool from the heat of his hands. . . . Now he has a slab of butter which has come straight from the refrigerator to make sure it is cold. He is pressing the butter slab flat. . . . Now he rolls out the paste to a large square and lays the butter on it."

Michel folded over the paste to envelop the butter. "Now he rolls out this 'sandwich,' " said Leighton, "and he folds it again. He continues to repeat this operation, folding and rolling, rolling and folding."

"The aim," said Michel, completely intent upon his task, "is to have all the layers of paste and butter thin and uniform. This is difficult to do and requires practice and concentration." He paused and looked up. "I am not stopping because I am tired," he explained. "It is to allow the paste to cool between turns. For perfect results, some chefs allow it to sit half an hour between rollings. Others put it into the refrigerator."

"Can I add a tip?" I asked.

"Certainly," said Michel.

"The rolling surface of the pastry can be quick-chilled with a self-sealing bag of ice. It is a trick used in hot climates."

Michel thanked me. Leighton hurried on.

"*Mille feuilles* means 'a thousand leaves,' " continued Leighton, "and you will get tired long before you reach that count." He looked around the room. "These tables are set up so that you can all try to make your own puff pastry."

Only a few minutes had gone by when the first loud groan came from one would-be pastry chef. "My arms are going to fall off!" she complained. Sympathetic noises sounded around the room. "There must be a machine for this!" said someone, and Leighton snapped, "There is—it's you." Another student grumbled. "I think this is just a sneaky way to get us to lose weight. I used to like pastry—not anymore."

Leighton and Michel were unrelenting taskmasters. "Nobody is born a chef," snapped Leighton to one protester. "You have to work to become one." Michel was supervising a different group. "No, no!" he was shouting. "You are pressing too hard. You do not want to blend the butter and the flour together. Each layer must be thin but separate."

It had been a good idea, I conceded, to leave this session until later in the week. The spa did not want to discourage its guests too soon, and there was no doubt that rolling *feuilletage* is difficult, tiring, and aggravating. I stayed with the class through its travails, lending a hand here and there.

"When do I graduate?" groaned one perspiring student.

Michel heard that. "You don't," he said. "You will be a student all your life if you work in a kitchen."

When everyone had finished, Leighton and Michel toured the tables, commenting on the results. Michel showed how to cut rounds and form them into cups. A large variety of fillings were on the tables—curly anchovy fillets, tiny shrimp in a pink sauce, chopped mushrooms with onions, ground turkey, foie gras, caviar, and several cheese blends. Some guests had chosen to make dessert soufflés: strawberry, cherry, orange, and blackberry were very apparent and all looked scrumptious. Tempers were being restored now and patience being recovered.

"The ovens are at four hundred and twenty-five degrees," Leighton said. "Your pastry will take fifteen minutes."

"Well done, all of you," said Michel, beaming.

Leighton was more reserved with his praise. "You've learned some of the tricks of making puff pastry, but it doesn't matter how beautiful it looks when it goes into the oven or when it comes out—if the taste is not there, then the dish is a failure."

A quarter of an hour later, Leighton's skepticism was justified. A foie gras pastry received frowns from both of the chefs—then, "Salt!" They both said it simultaneously. "It lacks salt." Accusing glances darted here and there, but no one stepped forward valiantly to claim responsibility and Michel gave a short but pointed speech on the need to check every ingredient. "Puff pastry is one of the most unforgiving dishes," he warned. "That is why it has such a reputation of being difficult to prepare. Certainly the baking operation is important, but it is critical to observe all the other aspects of preparing it."

Other pastries received nods of satisfaction, and some got words of approval. There was a chastened air about the guests who filed out after the session, but I caught a few comments that showed that many had gained a heightened respect for professional chefs and a better understanding of the demands placed on them.

CHAPTER TWENTY-FOUR

Switzerland's neighbor, Austria, was for centuries a crossroads of Europe. The great valleys of the Danube River provided ready-made passage for traders and merchants, linking East and West. From Roman times, what is now Austria has been host—even if sometimes unwillingly—to a variety of nations.

The Roman fortress of Vindobona became Vienna, and when Charlemagne's empire was divided among his grandchildren, Austria was the leading country in the Holy Roman Empire. From that time on, the history of Austria was the history of the Hapsburg family, and the country gained control of Hungary, Belgium, Sardinia, and much of northern Italy.

Karl Wengen was telling us all this. He was not only a politician but a renowned historian, it emerged, and his interest in history extended to many of its facets, including food.

Lunch was being served, and, the menu announced, this meal and dinner would feature Austrian specialties. This is what prompted Karl Wengen to give us a brief history lesson and explain why both the lunch and dinner menus today would contain dishes that were not only from Austria but also from its former possessions such as Hungary, Italy, and Bohemia and even former enemies such as Turkey.

I had the *porkolt*, which is thicker and contains more onions than the more familiar Hungarian goulash. Karl Wengen and a couple of others at the table had the *szekelygoulash*, another variation made with pork and sauerkraut. We all drank a light and pleasant Austrian white wine, a Veltliner from the Gumpold-skirchener district in the south of the country.

After the meal, I chatted with Marta, starry-eyed as usual. "Do you have any assignments for me?" she asked eagerly.

"Now, Marta, I told you I didn't come here to investigate," I admonished her.

"Isn't that what you have to say? So that no one knows you're under cover?"

"Which movie does that come from? That Charlie Chan one you were in?"

She gave me a mock glare. "Charlie Chan! I'm not old enough to have been in any of those."

"I think it was the last one," I said hastily.

"And I was too important a star," she added.

"I must have been thinking of that one with Cary Grant."

She softened. "Oh, yes, I was very good in that."

"I enjoyed it. You shouldn't have betrayed him, though."

"Why not?" she demanded indignantly. "He kept lying to me."

"I was disappointed in him there."

"I helped him. I could help you as well."

I decided not to remind her that she had got the signal wrong in that film. As a result of her pulling the wrong ear, the detective had arrived prematurely and caught Cary with the jewels in his hands.

"I'm sure you could," I told her. "In fact, you can help me . . ."

"Yes?" she said eagerly.

"By keeping your eyes and ears open."

She showed her dissatisfaction with that suggestion by using her expressive face. "Is there anyone you suspect? Oh, it doesn't matter, I know what you're going to say. You suspect everyone. At least, that's what Sidney Toler said."

Naturally, I did not give her any clue that she had made a gaffe.

Outside, I strolled across the grass. A good breeze was rolling up the valley but it was not bringing any sounds of cowbells. The sky was light blue and laced with disappearing vapor trails. Without making my way there in an obvious manner, I headed for the kitchen. No one was in sight except for a distant figure, and I slowed until the figure was gone. I tried the kitchen door. It opened.

Three of the younger members of the staff were in there. Their slightly stained white uniforms indicated that they had been responsible, in part at least, for the lunch. I looked around and satisfied myself that Leighton Vance was not here.

Two of the staff were young women, cleaning up. The third was a boy about twenty, and he had his arms full of large iron pans.

"Everyone at my table wanted me to congratulate you on the great Austrian dishes," I said heartily.

"Mr. Vance doesn't allow guests in the kitchen," said the boy, a little truculently.

"Oh, that's all right," I assured him. "He knows me."

The boy eyed me uncertainly. He had obviously had his instructions from Vance, but he also knew better than to argue with a guest. I waited for the pans in his arms to get heavier. They did. He went on with his task of returning them to their hooks on the far wall.

The girls were less concerned about spa protocol and one smiled shyly. "I had the *porkolt* and it was wonderful," I told her. "That flavor . . ."

"I made that," said the shy girl, a blue-eyed blond-haired Swiss miss.

"It deserved a prize," I told her. "Two people said it was the best they had ever tasted." That was only a slight exaggeration. I was sure I could have gotten two diners to endorse the statement, perhaps more.

"I made the goulash," said the other girl, a few years older and not quite as blond.

"I wish I'd had the goulash as well," I told her, and she glowed.

If Leighton allowed no contact between cooking staff and guests, these girls did not get much credit for their efforts, not from guests and probably not from Vance. I troweled on some further praise. It was not forced and certainly not insincere. I congratulated them on other dishes, but when I mentioned the *egli*, the fish dish, one of the girls said, "Oh, Mallory prepared that."

"What about Mr. Vance?" I asked, keeping my tone conversational. "What are his specialties?"

The girls glanced at each other in apparent embarrassment. Neither seemed to want to answer my question.

"I know pork tenderloins and soufflés are two of them," I prompted them.

The younger girl giggled. The older of the two gave her a reproving look.

"He cooked both of them for us at the cooking sessions," I explained.

They exchanged looks again, then the older girl said, "Yes, he is very good at both of those." She said it in a guarded way, but the other, less inhibited one now spoke out boldly.

"He should be good at them. He spent the whole week before, practicing them."

I digested that. I nodded. "All great chefs keep practicing their art," I told them.

I chatted with them a few minutes longer until the boy completed his pan handling. He had the facial expression known as a glower, and though I could have won him over with about two compliments, I didn't want to cause any trouble for the girls.

I left wondering why a chef of Leighton's caliber needed to practice. I also wondered again why he was adamant about keeping guests out of his kitchen. What happened there that he was so determined to hide?

The afternoon's sessions started with one conducted by Axel Vorstahl. He spoke on "the creative chef," and I listened from the back of a packed room. His excellent talk was well summarized by his opening statements. "Here, we cannot teach you how to be creative. What we do is teach you what you need to know so that you can be creative. We want to help you reach the position where you can make better use of your imagination and originality—two qualities that really stand out in cooking when fully demonstrated."

All of us combined for a succeeding presentation, which described the various cooking methods and explained when each one could be employed to the best advantage. As Michel pointed out, "sauté," "broil," "bake," "roast," and "grill" each has its own advantages and disadvantages. This was a visual session wherein the pans and utensils for each process were demonstrated and the materials of which they were made were compared.

It was an informative and undoubtedly useful presentation. Questions were asked and expertly answered, but the audience acceptance was at a lower level than at any of the preceding assemblies. I decided that a vital ingredient was lacking. It was an ingredient that all the other sessions had had, and that was food. Caroline was present, and I saw her making notes, presumably for elimination or at least improvement.

We concluded at about four-thirty, and as we were leaving the room Elaine approached me. "Not quite as much fun without something to eat at the end of it, is it?" she asked.

"You noticed that too, did you? Yes, I saw Caroline de Witt making notes. I think she felt the same way you and I did. Having pots and pans described and being told how to use them are important, but it lacks gustatory impact."

We walked outside, where the air was cooler than before. Wispy white clouds were drifting at altitudes below the tops of the visible Alps, and the sun seemed diminished. When we reached a quiet spot, Elaine stopped and turned to me.

"I found a message in my box this morning. It told me to phone a local number at one this afternoon. I did and a woman's voice invited me to a meeting."

"Someone you know?" I asked.

"Kathleen Evans."

CHAPTER TWENTY-FIVE

K athleen!" I gasped. "But she—"

Elaine pounced on my involuntary reaction. "Go on. She what?"

It was confession time. A more accomplished liar could have squirmed out of the predicament, but I was never that good with "terminological inexactitudes," as Winston Churchill once called them.

I looked around to make sure that no one was within earshot. "I didn't tell you everything," I admitted.

"Tell me now."

"I told you that I had a meeting with Kathleen in the Seaweed Forest—"

"A meeting?"

I had been through this before, explaining to Janet. I had withheld the most crucial part then, but now it was time to divulge it. "She asked me to meet her there—"

"Did she say why?" Elaine's questioning was becoming more like an interrogation. Her tone was sharper and her manner more aggressive. I felt like a transgressor who feels relief at confessing and finally being able to unburden himself.

"She didn't give any particular reason, no."

Elaine nodded. "Go on."

"When I got there, she was slumped against the weeds. I thought she was dead."

That slowed her down. "Dead? Why did you think that?"

"Her face was flushed. Her eyes were closed and her mouth was open. Those are symptoms of asphyxiation. She didn't move even when I took her arm."

"Did you feel for a pulse? Check her respiration?"

"I was doing so when I heard a sound, like someone moving very close by. I had heard it already, while I was looking for Kathleen. Just as I was about to try to find a pulse, I heard it again, much closer. Then there was a voice."

"Male or female?"

"I couldn't tell."

"What did it say?"

"Nothing I could distinguish."

"What did you do then?"

"I phoned reception. Told them to send someone at once to the Seaweed Forest, that there had been an accident."

Elaine was studying me, trying to determine how much of this was truth. I didn't think there was much in my story to doubt—it sounded too improbable.

"When was this?"

"The day you arrived."

She frowned. "There was no alarm, no commotion, no authorities—nothing?"

"Not a sign to indicate that anything had happened."

She digested that before murmuring, "That is very strange, very strange indeed."

"It certainly is. Maybe whomever the sounds and the voice came from were just innocent users of the Seaweed Forest, but I wasn't going to stick around and be proved wrong."

Elaine studied the sky with its fast-moving, thin white clouds. "It's too unlikely a story," she said. "It must be true."

"Of course it's true," I said indignantly.

"Well, don't be so high horse—you didn't tell me all this before."

"Would you tell a story like that to someone you didn't know well?"

Her mouth twitched in a near smile. "I wouldn't say we don't know each other well. . . ."

Some psychologist said that human relationships were never equal—that at all times, one or the other was dominant. Which way was it tilting now? I wondered.

"Why are you telling me about this?" I asked. "Why don't you just go and meet Kathleen, see what she has to say? No reason not to, you didn't even know there was a possibility of her being dead when you got her message."

"Because she specifically said you and I should come together. Otherwise, she wouldn't show up."

"Ah, and here I thought you were just being honest with me."

"I am being honest."

"Not altogether," I said. "For instance, why did Kathleen contact you? You already knew each other, didn't you?"

I recalled seeing the two of them in close conversation on the day of Elaine's arrival so this was something of a shot in the dark. It didn't score a bull's-eye, but it was inside the target area.

"We didn't exactly know each other but I knew her name and it turned out from our conversation that she knew mine."

"In what context?"

Elaine hesitated slightly, obviously trying to decide how much to tell me.

"So much for mutual honesty," I said, hoping the jibe

might prompt her to be impetuous, but I should have known better. Impetuosity was not one of her weaknesses. She did answer though.

"It involves that case I was telling you about—"

"The one you described as being a murder in a restaurant?"

She nodded as if reluctant to answer but then she said, "We can identify it that way for now. Yes, that's the case."

"So what's your connection with Kathleen?"

"She was proposing to do a story on it. The possibilities were considerable—a book perhaps, TV . . ."

"I see." Things were beginning to fit together. "So you think she may have been murdered because of something she knew concerning this case?"

"I didn't know Kathleen had been murdered. I knew she had checked out very unexpectedly and taken a flight out."

I felt deflated. I was not the only one ferreting out such information. Elaine went on, "She had flown here from New York with a stopover in Paris, so if she was returning, it was most likely by the same route."

"But she is not back in her office, and they are surprised that she is not still here at the conference," I said.

"Right," Elaine agreed.

"You know?"

"Yes."

"You called her office too?"

"Of course."

I was still mulling over this latest development. "You're certain it was Kathleen you talked to?"

"I couldn't be sure. I only talked to her that one time here at the spa, and voices can sound different on the phone."

"Where does she want us to meet her?"

"At the Hotel Goldener Hirsch in the village."

"Today?"

"Tonight at seven o'clock."

"Any idea where the number is you were told to call?"

"I checked it, obviously," she said in a voice that implied she wasn't exactly an amateur. "It was a call box in the village."

"So?" I asked. "Are we going?"

She checked the sky again. Presumably she obtained no meteorological inspiration. "What do you think?"

"I say let's go."

"Okay." She nodded firmly. "I'll order a taxi for six-thirty."

"I'll meet you in reception."

Elaine wore brown slacks and a brown sweater with a striped brown-and-white scarf. The heavy brogues looked like suitable Alpine climbing gear, and a few minutes before six-thirty I was perusing the people in the lobby. I hadn't completely gotten over my paranoia about the staff. My near misfortunes involving Rhoda of the blond staff beauties made me suspicious that some kind of cover-up would best be organized by the management but that had queries against it too. Certainly, the reception area was placid and innocent looking.

We had exchanged looks but no more when she had arrived a few minutes after me. We were now taking it in turns to watch for the arrival of one of the distinctive silver gray taxis. I relinquished my patrol and picked up a copy of the *Herald-Tribune*. I went looking for a place to sit and read it, or so I hoped it would appear. Elaine left the gift rack of ties, scarves, and trinkets to saunter past the big double glass doors. She turned her head and gave me a barely perceptible nod, then walked out. I gave the impression of having spotted a chair near the doors and went that way, then dropped the newspaper on to it and went swiftly outside to join her.

As we pulled out of the long driveway on the spa property and swung on to the highway, I looked back. "Nothing in sight," I murmured. She gave me a look that said she didn't expect any pursuit, and I reminded myself that she didn't know of the dangerous Rhoda. We settled down to the twenty-minute ride into Obergarten.

It was a typically pretty Swiss Alpine village. Upon arrival, I had passed through it but had little chance to see much. At this time of the evening, such activity as the place possessed was already slowing down, and shutdown would probably be complete within the hour. Shutters were going up over storefronts and shades were being pulled down. A horse and buggy trotted by, clattering over the centuries-old cobbles, its day of service to the tourist industry ended. Baskets of flowers hung on buildings and lamp standards.

The Town Hall flew the Swiss flag and the flag of the canton. Six wide steps led up to its ancient wooden doors, reinforced with black iron. Next to it, the Goldener Hirsch was the only hotel in the village, although a few guest cottages had signs at street corners.

"We're a few minutes early," Elaine said, looking at an intricately decorated clock mounted over the hotel entrance. "That is, if that clock is right."

"This is Switzerland," I reminded her. "Swiss clocks are always right. Let's look in a shop window or two. Reconnoiter the street."

We looked at glistening chocolates, women's clothes, kitchen appliances, hi-fis, and TVs. I was keeping an eye on the street, but everyone looked Swiss and honest without a doubt. As the hand on the clock slid past the hour mark, Elaine and I looked at each other and went in the main entrance of the Goldener Hirsch.

The small lobby had a thick carpet and dark wood paneling. A monstrous grandfather clock ticked loudly, maps and old paintings covered the walls. At the desk, an elderly dignified-looking gentleman was reading a newspaper. He gave us a glance to see if we needed attention and, deciding we didn't, went back to his paper.

We walked through a narrow corridor with old photographs on both sides. The restaurant looked cozy, with gleaming white tablecloths, cutlery, and glasses glinting from the shaded wall lights. It had a few people in it and a waiter approached us. We told him "not at the moment," scrutinized the faces at the table, and moved on to the Bierstube. Smells of beer and tobacco mingled companionably, but the only occupants of the room were four elderly men in lederhosen, playing cards at a table before the massive unlit fireplace.

The guest rooms were all upstairs, and after a glance up the steep staircase, we went on past the kitchen, which emitted odors of roasts and stews, and into a lounge where a television set was showing a German cops and robbers program. The sound was low, and the pistol shots muffled. The only occupants of the room were a young man and woman drinking wine in an upholstered corner booth. They looked up in what might have been guilt but resumed holding hands as we turned to leave.

"It's still only a few minutes after seven," I said.

Elaine made a sound, easily interpreted as meaning she was intolerant of unpunctual people. We strolled around and checked all the rooms again. No change was apparent. Elaine clucked her teeth in exasperation.

"We could have a glass of wine," I said hopefully, but

Elaine said, "We might be in the wrong room if we did that. Better wait in the lobby."

The elderly concierge gave us another glance; this time it lingered. "We're waiting for a friend," I told him, and he nodded. We took two of the basketwork chairs and sat. Time went by. Elaine drummed fingers in impatience. A red-faced man came in, exchanged a few words with the man at the desk, and went through to the restaurant. More time passed.

A wall clock over the reception desk read twenty minutes to eight. Elaine glared at me and sighed heavily, shifting in the uncomfortable chair. She was about to speak when the door opened. A woman came in and headed for the staircase going up to the rooms. She was heavily built and wore an old thick woolen coat and a hat in the Alpine style. She went up the stairs and all was quiet again.

"She's stood us up," Elaine said grimly. "Let's go."

I gave the old man at the desk a nod as we went out the door. "Should have asked where the taxi rank is," grumbled Elaine as we started out along the street, which was now quiet and empty. A car came around the corner and slowed. In front of the hotel stood a row of large-diameter iron posts, set in the edge of the concrete sidewalk so as to prevent parking. On the other side of the street was a row of spaces with meters. As the car turned into one of them, I grabbed Elaine's arm and pulled her into a shop doorway.

"What are you—," she was starting to ask angrily.

"Shh!" I said, and was glad she was fast on the uptake. We saw the car door open, and a tall blond girl climbed out. I watched as the girl crossed the street and came toward the Goldener Hirsch. At the entrance, though, she turned and went along the sidewalk with clicking heels. Near the far street corner, she stopped and knocked at a door. It opened, she said a few words, and went in.

"What's the matter with you?" Elaine asked angrily. "Do tall blondes always have that effect on you?"

"That one does," I said. "She tried to kill me. Maybe twice."

A few blocks away, we found a busy, noisy *bierkeller*. "Safety in numbers," I said, and we went down wooden stairs to a long room that sounded to be the loudest. We found a corner bench that nobody else wanted because it was too small. The room was full of students who, it seemed, were from Austria. The busload of them packed the room and they sat at long communal tables with tall steins of beer in front of them. They were laughing and shouting, arguing and disagreeing over everything but maintaining their good nature. They glanced curiously at us but quickly forgot we were there. The beamed ceiling was low and contributed to the din.

Elaine had to raise her voice. "So what else haven't you told me? About tall blondes?"

I told her about Rhoda delaying me when I was on my way to meet Kathleen in the Seaweed Forest and how I suspected that it had been during that delay that Kathleen had been flagellated to death and asphyxiated.

"Except Kathleen wasn't found when you reported this."

"True," I agreed. "But there's more. . . ." I told her about the incident in the mud bath and the temperature going up to the danger level. I described how Anita and Marta had saved me.

"Anita?" Elaine asked.

"Another of the blond beauties."

"And Marta? Oh, yes, the ex–movie star."

A dirndl-clad waitress with her hair in long pigtails was pushing her way through the clusters of students, nodding as she accepted orders for more beer. I ordered two steins also. Elaine shook her head. "You certainly live an exciting life. I thought you just detected foods? Are you sure you're not moonlighting?"

"And risking my life?" I said indignantly. "Certainly not."

"So you suspect this blond bimbo is involved?"

"It looks that way. The trouble is, I can't figure out what she's involved in."

Elaine didn't answer immediately, which prompted me to say, "Maybe you can, though. Maybe this is part of your investigation."

"No," she said, almost reflectively. "I don't see how it can be."

The students grew more rambunctious, but that mood phased quickly into some mournful college songs. The sound intensity mounted, and the low roof bounced the unmusical singing back at us. "This must be the college football team," Elaine said. "It's certainly not the choir."

We drank most of the beer, then I paid for it and we went out into the cool night, where the silence was deafening. A small square stood in front of what we found to be the railway station, and three taxis stood there. Only one driver was present, sitting on a bench smoking a cigarette.

I signaled to him, and he nodded, put out his cigarette, and came to the car. I opened the door for Elaine and I heard her let out a gasp. "The lady said she was waiting for you," the driver said in German, unconcerned. "Is that all right?"

In the back of the cab sat a muffled figure. I climbed in after Elaine. We sat side by side on the wide seat, Elaine in the middle. "The lady," as the taxi driver had called her, looked vaguely familiar and I leaned forward to get a better look at her. The cabbie got in and started the motor.

"The lady" took off her hat.

It was Janet Hargrave.

CHAPTER TWENTY-SIX

"I don't have to introduce you two, you've already met," I said. The women were eyeing each other warily. The driver broke in to ask us where we wanted to go. Neither Elaine nor Janet responded, so I said, "The airport." He flipped on the "occupied" light and we drove out of the village.

"Lots of explanations are due," I said. "Who wants to start?"

Elaine was equal to the challenge. "I will," she said, turning to Janet. "Why did you ask to see us?"

Janet was pulling off a heavy scarf that was wrapped around her waist. It was partly why she had looked so heavily built when she had come in to the lobby of the Goldener Hirsch and headed up the stairs. No wonder I had not recognized her, between that and the hat, which had concealed her face.

"First, I owe you an apology," Janet said to me.

"Oh? Why?"

"When I found myself locked in the herb garden glasshouse and those toxic fumes filling the place, I thought it must have been you who set me up."

I was trying hard to avoid Elaine's accusatory gaze, but it was impossible in the backseat of the taxi. The gaze was accompanied by demanding tones. "Glasshouse? Toxic fumes? What's all this? Can one of you explain?" If a cat were able to speak, these were the tones it would use while deciding whether to have the canary fried or tartar style.

"I was going to tell you," said Janet to me, "about Kathleen. That's why I asked you to meet me in the herb garden. I heard someone moving and went into the glasshouse to see who it was, just in case it wasn't you. The next thing I knew, a spray of anesthetic hit me from behind. Before I could turn, I passed out. When the anesthetic wore off, the fumes were filling the place. I tried to get out but couldn't.""

Elaine's lips were pursed tighter than a Scotsman's sporran. "Go on," she said icily.

"Well, I must have passed out because the next thing I knew, a blast of cold air blew over me and I recovered enough to sit up."

I couldn't wait to get in my quarter's worth and exonerate myself at least in Janet's eyes. "I tried to get you out of the glasshouse but I was too weak. I saw a power lawn mower among the equipment—one of those you sit on and drive. I crashed it through the glass wall—that must have been the cold air that revived you."

Janet managed a slight smile. "Thank you for saving my life, but of course I didn't know that at the time. It could have been you who set me up—you knew I was going to be there. I crawled out, and when I recovered my senses I decided to get as far away from there as possible. I got my things and checked out right away."

I gave Elaine a meaningful "there you see—I saved her life" look. She ignored me, concentrating on Janet. "What was it you wanted to tell him about Kathleen?"

Janet looked from one to the other of us. To Elaine, she said, "What's your role in this?"

Elaine was brief. She told of running across a law case concerning a murder in a restaurant and how it influenced her decision to become a lawyer specializing in cases dealing with food, ". . . a growing field and hardly any law firms in it yet."

"So why did you come here to the spa?" asked Janet bluntly.

"I had already decided to take a few weeks off before going into practice," Elaine said. "I thought a cooking course would give me some useful background. I checked out a few courses and several were at spas. I had no intention of starving myself on diets or having to do a lot of silly exercises. This place sounded ideal."

It sounded very convincing. So why did I feel a twinge of skepticism? I was about to ask a question but Janet beat me to it. "How did you meet Kathleen?"

"In the Manhattan Law Library. I was researching this case dealing with murder in a restaurant and she was there researching something too."

Lights blazed in the sky across the windows of the taxi. The roar of jet engines removed any possibility of conversation as an aircraft passed low overhead to land at the airport. The driver turned in to the entrance and slowed as he turned, pulled open the window between us, and asked, as he probably asked a dozen times a day, "Which airline?"

None of us replied, then I said, "Swissair."

He drove on a short distance, stopped, and we alighted. I paid him and he drove away. I watched to see if any vehicles behind him were stopping. None were.

"Why Swissair?" asked Elaine.

"It's the busiest," I said. "Let's go in and talk."

By the time we all had cappuccinos on the table in front

of us, Elaine had mellowed marginally and Janet was clearly glad to have allies. I opened the inning.

"Why did you come here to the spa after Kathleen?"

Janet nodded. "I expected you to ask that. It was the day Kathleen left. Later in the afternoon, I had a call from the credit card company. You see, Kathleen has a company card and also a personal one, both with the same company. There was some confusion over her card numbers and the company said did she really want this trip charged to the company account when all her previous trips had been on her personal account. Naturally, I said 'All her previous trips?' and they said they meant all her previous trips to the spa."

"Didn't you know she had been here before?" I asked.

"I knew she had been here once to do a story on them, but that was a while ago," Janet answered.

"She told me she had been there 'once or twice,' " I said, "but then in a later conversation with Tim Reynolds, the golfer, she said 'a few times.' "

"She was here six times," Janet said, "in the past four years. Except for that first time, she paid for the trips herself. I was very curious." She allowed herself a tiny smile. "I don't pay her the kind of salary for that."

"What was the story she did on this place?" I asked.

"She didn't complete it. Said it wasn't working out."

"Yet she was here again on this occasion, and if it was business," said Elaine pointedly, "then you must have known about it."

"She said she had new information that would enable her to pick up on the previous effort and, this time, write a major story."

"Didn't you want to know more?" Elaine demanded.

"I asked her. She didn't want to tell me—but you have to remember that she is a well-established writer. I never crowded her. I let her run her own stories."

"When you contacted Elaine, why did you give her Kathleen's name?" I asked.

"In case I was being followed, I wanted to cause some confusion. I certainly didn't want it known that I was still here. I had come to the airport to lay a false trail, then gone back to Obergarten."

"So where is Kathleen now?" asked Elaine in her unabashed way.

Janet sipped her cappuccino. When she had set her cup back in the saucer, she seemed reluctant to answer. She suddenly looked sad and forlorn. She said in a soft voice, "I'm very much afraid something has happened to her. Because of what she knows."

I could feel laser beams swiveling in my direction but it was only Elaine. "You'd better tell her," she said, and left me in the firing line.

I told Janet the whole story of the encounter in the Seaweed Forest. She asked all the same questions that Elaine had asked—why did I think she was dead? who else was in there? did I have any idea what Kathleen wanted to tell me and all the others?

Janet shook her head. "I'm afraid this confirms my worst fears." She looked at Elaine and I in turn, and her voice was despairing. "But why? What could she know that someone is afraid of? And who—is it someone here at the spa?"

"When you checked it out," I asked her, "why did you come here to Obergarten?"

"I was determined to find out something. I checked into the Goldener Hirsch."

"Have you been here all the time?"

"No. A woman was making inquiries about a woman she said was her cousin. It made me uneasy, so I checked into a guesthouse. I saw her again in the village and decided I'd be safer back at the hotel now that she'd checked it out, so I moved back."

"Good thinking," I complimented her.

"Oh, the inquiries may have had nothing to do with me, but I was nervous."

"This woman who was making inquiries," I said casually, "did you see her?"

"I caught a glimpse of her the first time. I saw her a little better the second time, when she was going to a guesthouse."

"Can you describe her?"

"I was more concerned about not letting her see me, but she was youngish, I think, tall, blond . . ." She broke off. My expression must have given me away. When Elaine saw this, she leaned forward and said in that chilly tone that I was beginning to dislike, "Your girlfriend, Rhoda, I presume."

Janet showed understandable alarm. "Girlfriend!" but I explained.

"That does suggest that the spa is directly involved," Janet said.

"Some of the guests are very regular and some of them spend a lot of time at the spa," said Elaine thoughtfully. "There is a possibility that one or more of them are involved."

"Which brings us back to the question, involved in what?" I said.

There was a brief pause, then Janet asked, "Do either of you know anything about the Glacier Caverns?"

CHAPTER TWENTY-SEVEN

The next morning was Friday and the final sessions of the course. After breakfast, everyone milled around, deciding which ones to attend. I was on the list for the session where favorite dishes, as requested during the week by the attendees, were to be prepared.

The previous evening we had eaten freshly caught trout after the cappuccinos. It was prepared in that carelessly brilliant way some chefs have, in this case with a sprinkle of herbs, a spoonful of cream and a shaving of shallot.

During the meal, Janet had told us that in one of her clandestine visits to the spa disguised as a portly old lady, she had seen the same blond girl who had been making inquiries in Obergarten, going up the trail that led to the Glacier Caverns.

"The brochure tells all about these," said Janet. "Several such glaciers can be found in various parts of the world, and there are a few in Switzerland."

"I've been in the glacier that is halfway up the Jungfrau from Interlaken," I contributed. "Rooms and chambers have been hacked out of the solid ice, right inside the glacier. It's an eerie experience."

"Isn't it freezing?" Elaine wanted to know.

"Surprisingly, no. It's cool but not excessively so. Ice is an insulator, so the interior stays the same temperature all the year. Outside it, though, seasonal changes and natural earth movements cause temperature shifts so that glaciers like that one and the one here are sliding downhill at several inches a year. These things are massive—several miles long and weighing millions of tons."

"The caverns here are temporarily closed," said Janet. "They are monitoring the slide, which they say shows signs of change. So they should not have been open the day I saw that girl going there."

"Could the Glacier Caverns have something to do with the mystery of whatever is going on here?" Janet asked.

"An illicit casino inside it?" I suggested facetiously, but neither of the women thought that funny.

"If something illegal is going on inside the caverns, would they still be having cooking classes at the spa?" asked Elaine skeptically.

"Today's the last day to find out," I said. "There are sessions all morning. If we're going to learn anything, it will have to be this afternoon."

"Let's talk—say, in the library at the spa," suggested Elaine. "Before lunch."

"I was on the phone to my office," said Janet. "I told them to go through Kathleen's files."

"Did they find anything?" asked Elaine.

"No, but one of the files needs a password, so I told them to bring in a computer expert to work on it. I'm calling in again this morning, so I may know more by lunch."

We saw Janet safely back to the Goldener Hirsch and listened to the large iron key turn in the lock, and then the assuring scrape of a bolt.

I was there early to prepare for my portion of the morning. I was finishing when the first of the eager students came drifting in.

Leighton Vance was first out of the starting gate in the sessions where I was to follow. As had been agreed, that perennial Swiss favorite, fondue, was the dish he was to demonstrate. He seemed pleased to be doing so, though I had thought that such a relatively simple dish would have been beneath him. His somewhat superior attitude suggested to me that he might have preferred to be cooking a more complex dish, but it could be that I was wrong about him. He went some way to proving that with his opening statement. . . .

"Fondue is widely known as a Swiss specialty, and we have had a great many requests for a practical demonstration on how to prepare it. It is a simple dish, but as with so many simple dishes, they are not always prepared properly. Here is the—*the* way to cook fondue." He picked up a large half-wheel of cheese and reached for a grater.

"I am taking cheese—Swiss cheese, naturally—and grating it finely," he began. "I am sprinkling flour on it and mixing," he went on, still grating. Then he took a heatproof earthenware pot, cut several garlic cloves, and thoroughly rubbed the inside of the pot with them.

"I pour in white wine—a Swiss white wine, naturally—and put it on this gas burner. I am heating it until it begins to bubble." He sprinkled in the cheese-flour mix, doing it very slowly and blending a little at a time. He kept stirring and adding until all the cheese was in. He then poured in kirsch, the cherry-flavored liqueur that is very popular in Switzerland and Southern Germany.

Bowls of crusty Italian bread cut into one-inch squares sat on the bench, and alongside them were long-tined fondue forks. "Now everyone take a fork," Leighton said, "while the fondue gets hot."

The aroma of the kirsch wafted through the air, for he had been very generous with it. Gradually, the cheese mixture began to simmer, large bubbles popping.

"Now when you spear a bread cube," warned Leighton, "be very sure that you penetrate the crusty side first—it stays on the fork that way. Some people keep the fondue melted over a hot-water bath, but a direct flame is much better as it forms a crust on the bottom of the pot, which greatly improves the flavor."

The rich smell of hot cheese had now devoured and replaced the aroma of the kirsch, and the large class was getting impatient to taste.

"Is the Italian dish that they call *fonduta* similar to this?" asked a voice.

"Not really," Leighton said. "The Italians add egg yolks and milk—no liqueur—and they spread it on toast squares."

The fondue was superb, and Leighton was complaining that it was eaten so fast that not enough time had elapsed to allow the buildup of a crust on the bottom of the pot. Now it was my turn, and I decided I had been too hard on the maestro. I was going to cook cheesecake, and surely it was not a dish to be snobbish about.

"We associate cheesecake with New York," I began, "and in New York, the famous Lindy's on Broadway always held the reputation of making the best. It was a great loss to the world of dessert lovers when the restaurant closed down, but I was among the fortunate few who managed to get the recipe.

"The moist chewy texture of the filling of Lindy's cheesecake was perfect, and the light golden crust was bursting with butter and sugar. If you like a cake that is light and airy, fluffy and spongy—you don't want this cheesecake. Lower-calorie and lower-cholesterol versions of cheesecake are plentiful, but they are not authentic. I am going to show you how to make the genuine Lindy's cheesecake, and you can introduce your own variations from there."

Faces looked expectant, and a few notebooks were poised.

I made the dough first, using only butter, sugar, vanilla, lemon rind, flour, and egg yolk. "Ideally, the dough should now be chilled for at least an hour," I pointed out, "but we'll chill this one just while I make the filling." I rolled the dough, spread it on a pan bottom, and put it in the refrigerator. I set the pastry oven at four hundred degrees.

I made the filling, combining sugar, flour, cream cheese, grated orange and lemon rind, and vanilla, and beat it well in the mixer. I added eggs and extra egg yolk, stirred in cream, poured the mix into a previously baked crust, and put it in the oven.

"I am baking at five hundred and fifty degrees for twelve minutes," I explained. "One of the secrets is to bake a further hour at low temperature—not over two hundred degrees. However, you don't want to wait that long to taste it, so I prepared one in exactly the same way earlier this morning. It's in the cooler and I'm taking it out now."

It was a magnificent sight. Rich and firm, dense but silky, and it was obvious that it was going to be indescribably delicious. "You will be able to smell the citrus flavors released from the orange and lemon rinds by the cooking," I said. "Inferior cheese-cakes can be detected at once by their weak aroma."

"You can put other toppings on it, can't you?" came a question.

"Cherry, strawberry, pineapple, blueberry are among the fruit toppings, yes. Though the dyed-in-the-wool cheesecake fanatics insist that those are just for tourists."

I had baked a large cake, large enough that there would be a good-size slice for everyone, and the consumption of this precluded any further questions. Millicent Manners was loud in her praise for a dish she said she never ate. Marta was near the front of the line and insisted on "only a half a slice," but while I was answering another question, I noticed her slipping back for "just a half."

By now, Michel Leblanc was there, making sure that everything was ready for his demonstration of how to cook cassoulet. It too was a great success, and the Frenchman had clearly had a lot of experience in preparing the dish, for he did so with great aplomb. Caroline de Witt came in near the end of Michel's session, and when he concluded she rapped on the table for attention.

"Many of you are leaving this afternoon, so lunch today will be the last meal of the course for you," she said. "We want to make it a special lunch, and so we are holding it in the Glacier Caverns." There were a few "oohs" and "ahs" at this. Caroline went on, "As you well know, the caverns have been closed, but we have permission to open the outer rooms on this occasion. Many have asked about seeing them, so you will want to take advantage of this opportunity. So please come along any time after twelve noon."

Her words drove all thoughts of Michel's cassoulet out of

my mind. Elaine was somewhere in the room, I knew, for I had glimpsed her during my presentation. I moved around in search of her.

Conversations were being conducted in twos and threes, and good-byes were being said. The room was filled with nostalgia and impressions were being exchanged. Elaine had caught my eye and we converged in a nearly empty spot. We were both circumspect about our reactions to Caroline's statement, for though the room was buzzing with voices, someone might move close enough to hear us.

"Will this make it easier or more difficult?" I murmured.

"Think positively," Elaine said in a soft voice. "Had anyone been watching us, he would have thought we were making an assignation."

"With so many people there, we may find it easier," I agreed.

"Yes. Let's hope it doesn't make it easier for them too."

I wished she hadn't said that.

CHAPTER TWENTY-EIGHT

Opinion among the guests was divided about the Glacier Caverns. Some found it hokey, and the name "Disneyland" was being bounced around at various levels of comparison. Others found it "delightful," while the universal adjective "interesting" was well to the fore.

Elaine and I had come early in case Janet was here already, but we saw no sign of her. The first chamber filled quickly and we viewed the exhibits. These were scenes from Swiss history and raised above the ordinary tableaux seen in museums and waxworks, as they were chopped out of the interior of the glacier—as was everything else.

The bluish translucent gleam of the solid ice statues gave them an unearthly look. Men, horses, weapons, flags, and standards were cut from the same frozen matrix of the glacier itself. The first displays showed a Roman legion marching out of an ice wall and represented the days when the Celtic people who settled in this region had first come face-to-face with the outside world when bronze-clad warriors of the armies of Rome came and subdued them. The glistening material from which they were chopped gave the legionnaires a ghostly reality.

In adjoining displays, giant statues towered twenty feet tall, and their names were cut into the ice pedestals: Theodoric, the great ruler of the Ostrogoths; Clovis, the Merovingian; Pepin; and the emperor Charlemagne. The mythical folk hero of Switzerland, William Tell, was the largest figure of all, dwarfing the tiny figure of his son, who was smiling in his evident faith in his father's marksmanship. Battle scenes from the Burgundian wars had phantom horses of ice, and a more peaceful scene depicted Martin Luther and the reformer Ulrich Zwingli.

More guests were coming in now. Gasps of awe ricocheted back from the high ceiling in tinny echoes. We walked into the second chamber, which was the size of a football stadium and filled with panoramic scenes from more recent Swiss history.

We stood inside the huge arch separating this chamber from the next. "See her?" Elaine asked. We stood for some time as more guests trickled in, but there was no sign of Janet. "Let's move on," Elaine said.

Switzerland's achievements in engineering occupied an enormous room: diesel engines and locomotives, aircraft and models of Alpine tunnels and bridges. Again, we looked for Janet, but there was no sign of her. Elaine and I were fascinated by a model of a hydroelectric installation above a massive dam. "Extraordinary, isn't it?" said a voice.

A cluster of guests were coming in behind us, and the comment came from the first of them, a woman with black hair and a pair of heavy black-rimmed glasses. Both Elaine and I were murmuring polite agreement and about to move on when the same thought occurred to us simultaneously. We both did a double take. The woman gave us a stare as icy as the vast chamber, and it froze any comment we might have made. We both looked at the woman again without making it obvious.

It was Janet.

She promptly looked away and walked slowly over to a display of agricultural equipment. It was not proving to be high in popularity, and when we strolled over to stand near her we were well out of earshot of the others. Anyone observing us would have taken us to be unacquainted as we chatted, seemingly strangers.

Janet wasted no time in small talk. "The expert broke Kathleen's password. She has been coming here to the spa, and the spa has been giving her free vacations."

Elaine asked. "Any clue as to why the spa would do that? Was she giving them publicity?"

"Quite the opposite, it seems."

"She was blackmailing them to give her free vacations," Elaine said. It was more of a statement than a question.

"It looks that way," agreed Janet.

"Blackmailing them about what?" I asked impatiently.

Janet was about to answer but Elaine took over calmly. "A restaurant called the Bell'Aurora at a resort in New York State." She looked at Janet. "Am I right?"

"Yes." Janet's eyes were flinty through the heavy black-rimmed glasses. "Where a husband-and-wife team of chefs were just becoming famous when a guest was poisoned. You're probably more familiar with this part," she said, turning to Elaine.

"Initially, the poisoning was thought to be accidental. Then it came out that a love triangle had existed between the husband, the wife, and a guest. There was a trial for manslaughter but the verdict was not guilty."

Janet nodded. "That's what you were researching at the Manhattan Law Library."

"So was Kathleen."

"She wanted to do a series of articles on husband-and-wife chef teams," said Janet. "She must have stumbled across this story in the course of her research."

I was determined to get in on this. "Whereas you," I said

to Elaine, "were intrigued with the legal potential of the food and restaurant business and came across the story of a poisoning in a restaurant. What I don't see is how that brought you here to the spa."

"Especially as the couple changed their names," added Janet.

It was a good thing that I was faster on the uptake in the field of food detection than in crime detection. The significance was only just beginning to sink in.

"Just a minute. Are we saying that Leighton and Mallory Vance are the chef couple from the poisoning at this place in New York?"

"Some of the notes in Kathleen's file include a local newspaper account of the trial. The names are different," Janet said.

"It's quite legal to change your name," said Elaine dismissively. "Also it's understandable that they would want to do so if they intended to pursue their career—and they obviously did, coming here to Switzerland."

"There has to be more to it than that," I said, musing. "A place as prestigious as this would need extensive references."

Neither of them answered. I wasn't sure whether either of them knew the answer or had some reason for not replying.

"There must be even more to it," I persisted. "Blackmailing for vacations? Sounds a bit weak. Certainly not enough motive for murder. So what's our next move?" I asked.

Still neither responded.

"Do we have a next move?" I wanted to know.

In the next room, a great ice table made a splendid setting for a farewell banquet, under a glistening dome of shiny blue ice. One wall was a faithful replica of the front of a medieval château, complete with moat, drawbridge, and portcullis. A sign in red was not legible from this distance but looked like a warning not to enter. The other walls had banners of the cantons and the national flag, with the familiar red cross on a white background.

Ice tables don't groan, so it could not be said that this one groaned under the weight of its spectacular spread of food, but it had every reason to do so. It was buffet style and was a mouthwatering selection that already was outweighing the glacial attractions of Swiss history, agricultural equipment, and Swiss engineering achievements. Guests were flocking round the table, and the rattle of cutlery on plates was like hail on the roof as it echoed down from the icy blue dome.

"The Swiss are so *boring* with their accomplishments," Oriana Frascati hissed to me as she loaded a plate with smoked salmon and tiny puff pastries filled with shrimp.

"You should speak more charitably of your neighbors," I reprimanded.

"Hitler should have listened to Mussolini when he wanted to invade Switzerland," Oriana said haughtily, reaching for cheese rolls made with four kinds of cheese.

Elaine had drifted away and was talking to Brad Thompson. Janet was trying to keep out of range of Caroline de Witt, who was presiding over the table like a benign duchess. We had discussed our next move, which it had transpired we did not have. Janet was adamant that she was not going to leave until she found out what had happened to Kathleen. Elaine and I agreed to keep an eye on her. Janet's sole clue was that she had seen Rhoda coming to the Glacier Caverns. That was suspicious only because the caverns were not supposed to be open at the time. Janet insisted she was going to look around now. She reminded us that the caverns were said to be extensive, so there must be chambers that we had not seen in our tour.

"What are these?" Marta Giannini demanded, waving me over.

I told her they were tiny crab cakes.

"What's that red in them?" she asked suspiciously.

"Flecks of red pepper."

She tasted one and promptly took another.

The blond staffers were moving through the crowd of guests, offering Swiss wine. It was from the Visperterminen in the Valais, the highest vineyard in Europe, and it was crisp and dry, more assertive than many Swiss wines. It was a good solution to the problem that has confounded many a hostess—which wine to serve with a buffet.

"You read the brochure," I said, motioning to the fluffy scarlet sweater that Marta was wearing. It was a dazzling garment, but I presumed it also had a practical purpose.

"It's not as cold here as I thought," she said, "but I am glad I wore it." She looked around carefully, making sure no one was near enough to overhear—just as she had in *Games in the Night*, when the will had just been read and a statue had fallen from above and only just missed her. "I do have a little more information for you," she said in a hoarse whisper that had "conspirator" stamped on it.

"Might be safer to talk in a natural voice," I said, trying not to put it in the way that director von Stroheim might have. "Less suspicious."

We were evidently on different cinematic wavelengths, for she nodded and said with a straight face. "Yes, Mr. Capra."

"So you've been sleuthing," I prompted her.

"I didn't have to. That Frenchman, Michel Leblanc, I know now what he and Kathleen Evans were talking about in the Roman baths and the other time, on the lawn."

"You do? What was it?"

"Your coarse American expression is the best way to put it. He 'came on to me.'"

"Can't blame him for that," I said, hoping it sounded gallant. If it did, she failed to notice. "Thinking back to those two times I saw them, I'm sure that's what he was doing then." She twirled her champagne glass and put on a Hollywood smile. "Don't say anything. Here he comes now."

Michel joined us, pointing to a toothsome array of tartlets on a glass tray. "I made those," he said proudly. "Baked oysters." We tasted and congratulated him.

Small triangles of pizza had broccoli *rabe,* black olives, and smoked mozzarella and were proving a popular item. Toasted cakes fresh from the oven and piled with goat cheese shavings were going like—well, like hot cakes.

I became aware of eyes on me from across the table. It was Elaine, and she was very judiciously flickering her gaze across the chamber toward the wall carved like a château front. I was just in time to see Janet disappear through the portcullis gate.

Eating and drinking stimulate my brain. Anyway, I have always gotten away with that story, and it seemed justified now. Janet's information clarified some of the mystery, but the whereabouts of Kathleen and her probable fate were still clouded.

"Puzzling over what to eat next?"

The question broke in on my thoughts. It was Leighton Vance in a snappy sky-blue blazer with an impossibly white shirt and white pants. He looked to be in a cheerful mood, and he was with Millicent Manners, uncharacteristically bucolic in a Tyrolean-style skirt and blouse.

"It's all so good," I said.

"A fitting farewell," he said with a smile. "Have you tried the spring rolls?"

"No, did you make them?"

"One of my staff did," he said, implying that making spring rolls was beneath his culinary dignity.

I tasted one. "An interesting variation on the Oriental way of making them."

He had already turned his attention back to Millicent Manners, and my compliment fell on deaf ears. I drifted along the table, stopping to exchange pleasantries with the Japanese lady and with Helmut Helberg, who was lamenting the end of the week having arrived so quickly. I continued to drift until I met Elaine, disengaging herself from Gunther Probst.

"That man wants to put everything on software," she complained.

I waited until we were in a comparatively safe zone, then said, "Did you see Janet? She went into the ice château."

"One second she was there, the next she was gone," Elaine said. "I assumed that's where she disappeared to. Are you going to follow her?"

"Me? Well, I suppose one of us should."

"You're the investigator," she said, elegantly crooking a little finger as she picked up a rib glistening with a reddish sauce.

"Actually, I'm not," I protested. "Like I told you, I only—"

"I know, I know," she said impatiently, "but you're the nearest thing to an investigator we have."

"Very flattering. I'm not sure what I can do, though."

"Have you tried one of these ribs? They're delicious." She was licking the sauce and it did look good.

"Venison, isn't it?"

"I don't know, but I'm having another."

"So while you're stuffing yourself, you want to send me into the jaws of death?"

"As a lawyer, I can't recommend prowling around where signs specifically prohibit such an activity. On the other hand, I don't see what else we can do. We have nothing to take to the police. One disappeared female, who for all intents and purposes has gone back to New York? They'd laugh at us—well, no, being Swiss, they'd be very polite—but where would that get us?"

"Are you sure that the best alternative is sending me in there? Well," I said, "it doesn't matter. If Janet is in there, I have to go in after her."

"Stout fellow," she said with only a touch of irony. "Only don't say 'I,' say 'we.' "

"You're coming too? I thought you were ducking out, sending me?"

"Just wanted to see your reaction. Anyway, first, I need more sustenance." She took another venison rib and I took one too. One of the blond staffers was nearby, pouring the very good Vesperterminen wine. Elaine and I both had refills, and I noted that the staffer's name badge said "Olga." "I haven't seen Rhoda today," I said to her. "Is she on duty?"

"She's on a few days' leave," the blonde replied.

She gave me a dazzling smile and continued on her wine-dispensing mission of mercy.

"I don't like the sound of that," I murmured to Elaine.

She didn't offer any solace, being too busy scanning the

scene. "Everybody's pretty well occupied right now," she said quietly. "We'll split up, go to the fringes of the crowd, one to the right, one to the left, then one at a time head for the château entrance."

"Portcullis."

"Whatever." She was gone, and I had just time enough to empty my wineglass before I moved too.

CHAPTER TWENTY-NINE

I'm not afraid of the dark—well, no more than the average person anyway. This was a different proposition, though: these Cimmerian chambers were deep inside the bowels of a glacier that was not only millions of years old but sliding downhill at the rate of several inches a year. I kept reminding myself that this was Switzerland, and the Swiss are too realistic, too practical, too efficient to permit dangerous places like sliding glaciers. Besides, they would affect the tourist business.

My worst fears, the ones about the dark, were not realized. A subdued yellowish light filled the chamber into which we passed. It was barely bright enough to read by but certainly bright enough to find one's way in, presumably a permanent installation fed from one of the country's many nuclear generators.

Elaine and I walked on cautiously. Despite our attempts at stealth, our footsteps echoed from the ice walls and even our whispers seemed to fly around like bats. The layout of a castle was continued after we had passed through the portcullis and the main gate. This was a large courtyard. The floor was cut to resemble cobblestones and the walls were buttressed. A horse and carriage stood frozen, literally, while wax figures in costume stood poised to carry out their tasks.

"I thought we would have caught up with Janet by now," Elaine murmured.

"So did I," I agreed. "We could hardly have passed her so she must still be ahead of us."

"Wherever that is."

A door at either end was our next consideration. The first one I tried opened readily and we went through into the main hall. Trusses and beams were cut from the ice, and the open staircase on one side seemed ripe for a duel to be won by Douglas Fairbanks or Errol Flynn. Even the massive chandelier was chopped from the ice and the minstrel gallery that looked down on the scene below lacked only a group of medieval musicians.

"Listen!" Elaine snapped out the word so abruptly that I almost jumped out of my skin. She was right, there was . . . something. It resembled voices but no words were distinguishable, and the echoes from the ice mangled the sound beyond identification. There was no choice of doors here, just one large one. Elaine shrugged, opened it, and went through.

"Glad you could join us!" called out a welcoming voice. "Come on in and have a glass of champagne."

It was a smaller room, though perhaps that was just the contrast from the spacious main hall. It was warmer too, because of the tapestries that hung all round the walls, screening off the chill from the ice. It was furnished like a luxurious club room, with carpets, large leather sofas and armchairs, small tables, and built-in wooden cabinets. It was brightly lit with floor lamps and overhead lighting.

"Cozy place you have here," I commented as Elaine and I sank into one of the comfortable leather sofas.

On the wooden table before us was a bottle of Dom Perignon in a bucket of ice. Leighton Vance and Caroline de Witt occupied armchairs opposite us. Leighton rose and went to the wall cabinet, returning with two fluted glasses. He placed them in front of us and poured. He carefully topped them after waiting for the foam to subside.

"What shall we drink to?" Elaine asked brightly.

There was a silence. Leighton picked up his half-empty glass and drank most of it.

"The end of the line?" he suggested.

I glanced at Caroline de Witt. She looked as regal as ever, calm and composed but not inclined to join in the conversation, it seemed.

"You know most of it already, don't you?" Leighton's voice was measured, his utterance more statement than question.

"No, we don't," I said quickly. "We don't know a thing. Just what are you doing down here? Brewing moonshine liquor? Plotting to overthrow the Swiss government? Forging thousand-franc notes?"

Leighton and Caroline looked at each other and laughed. Caroline drank some more champagne. "What are we doing down here?" chuckled Leighton. "Caroline and I? What a dreadfully gauche question!"

Elaine was less than amused. Her voice was a little touchy when she said to me in what was almost an aside, "It's a love nest, we realize that." To Leighton, she went on, "We also know that your real name is Lionel Fenton, and you are the former owner of the Bell'Aurora, a restaurant in northern New York State, where a dinner guest died from eating poisoned mushrooms."

Neither Leighton nor Caroline reacted, but the silence was significant.

"Is that what this is all about?" I demanded. "You were accused of manslaughter but found not guilty. Kathleen Evans found out about it and blackmailed you into giving her free vacations here. You killed her in the Seaweed Forest and disposed of her body. . . ."

Leighton and Caroline exchanged laughs again. Leighton slapped his knee. "We murdered a magazine columnist over free vacations! That's a good one!" He pointed to Elaine. "Your learned friend knows better than that."

I looked at Elaine. She was torn between wanting to tell everything she knew and avoiding saying anything that might endanger our already precarious position. It would be a tough choice, I could see that in her face. I hoped she would decide correctly. Leighton didn't know her as well as I did, and he misinterpreted her hesitation.

"You'd better tell him," Leighton continued, still looking amused. "Accusing me of manslaughter, indeed! What an awful thing to do! Isn't that grounds for slander?"

Caroline was joining in the amusement now, her red lips parted in a wide smile. All this joviality pressed Elaine into making up her mind.

"It wasn't Leighton who was accused of poisoning the guest at the Bell'Aurora," she said, not just to me but to the room at large. "He didn't stand trial for manslaughter. It was Mallory."

I was determined not to indicate any dissension in the ranks so I didn't ask Elaine accusingly. "Why didn't you tell me?" Elaine was aware that the words were on my tongue, though, and she said, mainly for my benefit, "I only just found out."

Leighton refilled his glass, shaking his head sadly. "It's hard for a man to keep something like this concealed for so long. I've kept quiet about it as far as I could but there comes a time . . ." He drank champagne with a flourish that illustrated drowning his sorrows.

"You'll feel better if you tell the whole story," I told him piously. "Confession is good for the soul."

Caroline spoke up for the first time. "I'd better tell it. Leighton milks it. He and Mallory had this restaurant, the Bell'Aurora. It was getting to be really popular. Leighton's partner, Edward Lester, had this crush on Mallory, wouldn't leave her alone. She didn't want to discuss it with Leighton—he has a jealous streak. She put some poisoned mushrooms in Lester's salad. Perhaps she only intended to give him a scare. That's what her lawyer said. Anyway, he died. Lester's infatuation with Mallory was well known to the regulars and the restaurant staff. Several of them gave evidence, and she was tried for manslaughter. Her lawyer was good. She was found not guilty."

"Mallory and I changed our names. We went to Canada, then to France, then came here to Switzerland." Leighton took up the story, not wanting to be left out. "Kathleen Evans found us by accident. She was planning a story on husband-and-wife chefs. She came across the story of the Bell'Aurora and linked it to us. Naturally, we let her stay here for free rather than have the story leaked."

"So you killed Kathleen to stop her from telling anyone you were here," I said indignantly. "Let's not lose sight of that!"

Caroline stretched back languidly in the big leather armchair. "It's Leighton's fatal charm. One of the girls has a passion for him—"

"Rhoda," I supplied.

"Yes," she said. "Rhoda turned the flagellation level up too high. We knew nothing about it until it was too late. We had to get rid of the body, of course."

"Then Rhoda tried to get rid of me," I reminded her. "In the mud baths. Fortunately, she failed."

"Did she really?" Caroline looked surprised. "The girl is very zealous, I know, but that was going a little too far."

"I couldn't agree more."

There was no keeping Elaine quiet for very long. "Tell us about Janet," she invited.

"We were surprised when she showed up here," Caroline said. "Presumably she decided to take up where Kathleen had left off."

"And where is she now?"

Leighton and Caroline looked at each other. Caroline was the first to answer.

"How would I know? I thought she had gone back to New York."

"Didn't I hear that she had checked out hurriedly and taken a cab to the airport?" asked Leighton in that offhanded manner.

I was baffled. This all sounded plausible. Could it be true? Could even part of it be true?

"You'll have to do better than that," I suggested, "or are you going to blame this on the murderous Rhoda too?"

Leighton shrugged as if he could not care less. Caroline was impassive.

"Well, if there's nothing more to be learned here, we might as well leave," Elaine said.

"True," I said, and rose. We both headed for the door. This would be the test, I thought. Would either of them make a move to stop us?

The door creaked as it opened. Elaine and I turned. We both stared at the man who walked in, but I wasn't looking at Elaine's expression. I was too astonished.

CHAPTER THIRTY

The newcomer nodded pleasantly to Leighton and Caroline. "Unexpected and late but nonetheless very welcome," Leighton said with a smile. "Do come in and have a glass of champagne."

"We wondered about you." Caroline's greeting was just as warm. "We thought you would be here, but when you didn't arrive, well, we just had to go ahead and run the week without you."

He was just under six feet tall, sturdy but not heavy, brown hair and brown eyes, and he moved lithely and confidently. I was still staring at him. Why did people keep saying I looked like him? I didn't really.

"What the devil are you doing here?" I demanded angrily.

Elaine cut through the proceedings with a voice like a scimitar. "Will someone introduce me?"

"Carver Armitage," Caroline obliged. "Elaine Dunbar."

They shook hands politely. Carver turned to me. "I'm supposed to be here, remember?"

"You *were*," I corrected. "You asked me to come in your place."

He eased himself into an armchair and immediately looked at home. It was one of his irritating characteristics. Leighton handed him a glass of champagne and he sipped it appreciatively.

"We missed you," Caroline said, "but we managed." She could have given me some credit for filling the gap, I thought, and gave her a further opportunity to do so, but when she failed, I tossed a little vinegar into the blend.

"I hope you are well enough to be traveling, Carver. Is it wise so soon after being released from hospital?"

Caroline and Leighton looked solicitous. "Hospital?" said Leighton, "I didn't realize that was why you weren't here."

"I presume the surgery was successful," I added, unwilling to relinquish the needle.

Carver basked in the wave of sympathy and treated my comment as part of it. He nodded in my direction. "Should have told you, I suppose. Fact is, I damaged a finger and went to St. Giles's Hospital for treatment. Trivial, I know, but very painful."

Caroline and Leighton made appropriately commiserating noises. I was trying to decide whether I believed him or if he was playing some devious double game. Only Elaine was stonily resistant to this syrupy compassion. "You have a food program, do you?"

"I do, indeed, and a daily column. I am also—"

Elaine didn't want a list of his credentials. She knew where she was going.

"If you're a columnist, you must know Kathleen Evans—and her editor, Janet Hargrave."

There was a stillness for just a couple of seconds. I glanced at Leighton and Caroline. They sat calmly, awaiting Carver's response.

"Of course. They are both here, I understand."

"They were," Elaine corrected him. "Both returned to their office earlier this week."

Carver drank champagne, gave a studied approval to the rising bubbles. "Actually, they didn't. Their office thinks they are still here."

Elaine flicked her gaze toward me, but I was waiting for the reaction of the man and woman opposite. Caroline twisted the stem of her glass between her fingers. She put the glass down. "We had rather that this subject had not come up," she said, "but since it has . . . I am sure you can understand that running an operation like this, we are susceptible to guests' opinions, especially those concerning other guests' behavior."

"I don't understand," I said bluntly.

"Two women, coworkers, perhaps unable to show their true feelings in the workplace. They share a room here, sense a resentment around them, decide to go somewhere else—"

"That's nonsense!" I burst out. "They didn't share a room here, they had different rooms."

"Our records show that they did share a room," said Caroline. Her large dark eyes were round and persuasive.

"We have more evidence than that." Elaine was loud and forceful. "Don't we?" she said to me.

"We do. Kathleen asked me to meet her in the Seaweed Forest—" I began.

"Just the two of you?" asked Caroline. "You and her?"

"Yes. When I got there, I thought she was dead. I went for help. . . ."

When I finished my story, the tension in the chamber had increased. "If she was gone and there was no alarm," said Carver, "presumably, she wasn't dead at all."

"There's more," prompted Elaine.

"There's a lot more," I said. "I went to the Herb Garden to meet Janet Hargrave—"

"My, my," Leighton commented. "You have been active. Maybe we should be concerned about his effect on our reputation too," he said, turning to Caroline. I ignored him and went on. When I came to the end, it was Carver again who said in a skeptical voice, "And her body had disappeared too?"

"That's right," Elaine said silkily, and I knew she had a purpose in agreeing so readily.

"Let me get this straight," Caroline said. "Two guests, you thought them both dead and both have disappeared."

"A good summary," nodded Elaine. "The difference with Janet, though, is that she really wasn't dead. She had been overcome by the fumes but the air rushed in when the glass wall was smashed and revived her."

"You've seen her since then?" Leighton asked, enunciating carefully.

"Oh, yes." Elaine's casual response should have been accompanied by a studied examination of her fingernails.

"So where is she now?" asked Carver.

Elaine said nothing, and I could sense her willing me to keep quiet too. The tension increased.

Carver addressed Caroline. "Didn't you say the two of them had left?"

"Apparently they both called cabs and went to the airport," Caroline replied, still as cool as ice.

"So if they've both left—"

"Janet is still here," Elaine said. "She was with us at the farewell luncheon today."

I was watching Caroline and Leighton as soon as I realized what Elaine was saying. Neither batted an eyelid, but the tension rose one more notch. Something had to snap soon.

For the first time since he had arrived, Carver looked less

than his normal composed self. "An attempt was made on Kathleen's life in the Seaweed Forest, you say? And another attempt on Janet in the Herb Garden?"

A silence greeted this review, but I saw it as having an affirmative overtone.

"Then where is Janet now?" Carver wanted to know.

Leighton and Caroline looked at us for a reply. We looked back at them.

"I know that neither of them is back in their office," Carver said. "When I called there yesterday, they certainly weren't, and no one had heard from them."

"Is that what brings you here?" I asked him.

"In a way," he said.

"More specifically," Caroline asked and was unable to keep an edge out of her question, "how did you find us here in the Glacier Caverns?"

"Mallory brought me." Carver tossed it out casually and reached for his champagne glass.

That brought the strongest reaction so far. Leighton leaned forward suddenly. He opened his mouth to say something but didn't. Caroline looked as if she wished she hadn't asked the question.

"Is Mallory here?" Elaine asked.

"We ran into some of the last people leaving the luncheon room," Carver said. "She stopped to talk to a couple of them." He emptied his champagne glass with an air of moving on to more important matters. "I did, in fact, have another reason for coming here," he said as he put his glass on the table.

"And what is that?" Leighton asked as if not sure that he wanted to know.

"The case has been reopened." Carver looked at us in turn.

"I'm sure we all know by now what case I'm referring to. A new trial is going be held, based on fresh evidence that has come to light. The charge this time is murder."

That brought the temperature down to the chilly region of the ice walls. Leighton was the first to speak.

"Poor Mallory," he said softly.

Then he asked, "Who else knows we are here?"

"Kathleen and Janet knew," Elaine said promptly. "That's why you wanted to kill them both."

"That's absurd," said Leighton. He turned to Carver. "You stayed here last year, which is why we asked you to participate in this event, but what's your interest in the trial?"

"Kathleen approached me with the idea of a story about husband-and-wife chef teams—"

"Why would she do that?" I interrupted. "She'd want to keep a story like that for herself."

My suspicions of Carver were resurfacing.

"Because after her first enthusiasm over the idea, Kathleen decided it would be even better as a TV series. The human story of a married couple, their rivalry in the same business, cooking on camera, perhaps trying to outdo each other in some specialties . . . She thought that my TV contacts would help pave the way at the studio"—he reflected for a moment—"well, they would, I suppose," he added in that supercilious way he has. He really isn't in the least like me.

"Go on," I said.

"I said I would work with her on it. She did more investigation and came across the story of the first trial."

"And how did you hear about the new trial?" asked Leighton.

"When I called Kathleen's office, they were getting so concerned about her that they asked me if this message from the Manhattan Law Library helped at all in locating her. Apparently, she had flagged this case so she would be informed as soon as anything new came in on it."

The heavy iron lock of the door rattled.

Mallory entered.

CHAPTER THIRTY-ONE

Leighton was out of his chair and hurrying to Mallory's side. He took her hand.

"My dear, come and sit down. You remember Carver Armitage from last year, don't you?"

She wore a simple blue dress, the blue of Alpine wildflowers. She had on plain white shoes and she looked pale, although that was perhaps the unaccustomed lower temperature of the Glacier Caverns after the heat of the kitchen.

She acknowledged Carver. He returned the greeting but was looking at her strangely. She began to look around the chamber, "the love nest" as Elaine had called it, and her gaze went to Leighton and Caroline. Some color came back.

In view of the revelations of the previous minutes, the awkward pause that followed was not surprising. Someone had to break it, and the intrepid Elaine was the most likely.

"We have to deal with realities here," she said briskly. "I'm sorry, Mallory, but the first reality is that we have one murder and one disappearance. I'm referring, of course, to Kathleen Evans and Janet Hargrave. Both appear to have had knowledge of the events at the Bell'Aurora, and I'm afraid this makes you the prime suspect."

Mallory nodded indifferently. I wondered if she had a mental problem and the unpleasant thought flashed through my mind that she might be schizophrenic. Could this quiet, gentle girl be a killer? None of our conversations had contained any hint of such a possibility, but the niggling doubt was there.

Mallory's next words gave it a chilling reinforcement.

"It's two murders. Janet is dead."

Carver gave a grunt of astonishment. Caroline's eyes widened, and she looked at Leighton. At first, he showed no emotion, then he began to shake his head sadly. Elaine must have been taken unaware but she did not display it. She was already in training for courtroom confrontations, I thought.

"Has there been some further news from Manaqua County?" Mallory asked, her voice still calm.

I looked at Elaine to see if this meant anything to her. She nodded and said for the benefit of those of us who didn't know, "The Bell'Aurora restaurant is in Manaqua County in upstate New York. Yes, there has been news. The case is being reopened and a date for a retrial is to be set shortly."

"A retrial." Mallory's voice sounded bemused but she appeared to understand. "It was for manslaughter before and you can't be tried for that twice. That means that next time . . ."

"Yes," Elaine said. "The new trial will be for murder."

"Mallory, how do you know Janet is dead?" Carver asked. He rose to his feet.

"Her body is in the next antechamber," Mallory said simply.

"Will you show it to us?"

Carver took Mallory by the arm, inviting her to lead the way. Leighton took her other arm and pulled her away and toward him. She went to the door, and we all followed.

I wasn't sure what we were going to find. Mallory's condition could mean she was having delusions. Perhaps her mind had finally snapped under what must have been a tremendous strain.

The antechamber was bare. There were alcoves chopped in the ice walls, evidently to serve as open storage cabinets. One contained tools and a wheelbarrow. Blankets were piled in others, and Mallory led the way toward them. I felt a profound melancholy and I could empathize with Leighton when he had breathed, "Poor Mallory" on hearing Carver give the news of the retrial.

But then she was pulling a blanket aside to reveal the face of Janet, white and still in death.

Elaine was the first to react. She carefully turned back the blanket further. We could see that the back of Janet's head had been smashed in.

"She could have fallen," said Carver.

"No," Elaine said definitively. "A blow, with something heavy."

Mallory spoke up unexpectedly, and her words floated in the cool air. "I took the blame for you at the Bell'Aurora like you wanted. They wouldn't convict me, you said, and you were right."

She was still staring at Janet's face, but all eyes turned toward Leighton as it became suddenly clear that Mallory's words were addressed to him.

"I've let you take the credit for my cooking all these years, and I've overlooked your affairs with Rhoda and with Caroline. I didn't put the poison in the mushroom salad at the Bell'Aurora. I served it, but you prepared it—it surprised me when you wanted to do that. But no more. This is enough. You killed Edward, not because he was always making advances toward me but because you wanted to take full control of the restaurant. You were always arguing with him about it. You used me as a screen for killing Edward, and I know you must have killed Kathleen Evans and now Janet Hargrave."

Her mildness was evaporating with every sentence, and her voice was rising. "So there's going to be a new trial! And this time for murder! Well, you'll be in the dock this time, not me! And the charge will be three murders!"

Leighton was looking at her, stunned. He managed a weak rebuttal. "Mallory, you don't know what you're saying!"

"I think she does." The statement came from Caroline. She had backed away from the group around the body of Janet, and she was taking a small automatic pistol from her purse. "Come on, Leighton, time to go."

He shook his head, still in shock, then stumbled toward her. She continued to back away toward another door, one with a large key in the lock. She turned the key with her free hand and pulled it out of the lock. She swung the door open and beckoned Leighton through. He followed like an automaton, clearly unable to believe Mallory's transformation.

The door slammed, and the key grated in the other side of the lock.

"We can't let them get away!" Elaine called out. "Where does this go?"

Mallory shook her head. "Tunnels go a lot farther into the glacier. They were intended to shelter hundreds of thousands of people if there was a nuclear war. But the canton says they're not safe any longer."

"What about that other door?" Carver asked.

"I'm not sure," Mallory said, shaking her head.

Elaine ran to it and pulled it open. "Come on!"

Carver looked at me uncertainly, then followed, as did Mallory and I.

A large tunnel stretched far out of sight. The subdued lighting made it just tolerable, otherwise none of us would have gone any farther. "Listen!" said Carver.

We listened. A faint clatter of footsteps could be heard, echoing down the tunnel.

"Come on!" Elaine said again.

We reached a bend sooner than we had thought, for the eerie whiteness of the ice walls blended into a uniform pattern that was deceiving. We went on, and a dull sound caused us all to pause. It was the sound of rushing water.

"Some parts of the glacier must be melting," I said.

"Where do they expect to go?" asked Elaine.

"There is an elevator," Mallory answered. "It used to go up to a ski station a long time ago, but it hasn't been used for ages."

The sound increased as we went on. "This is crazy," Carver protested. "What can we hope to do?"

"We can't let them get away," Mallory said, and in the icy air her face was grim and set. Phrases about "a woman scorned" came into my head, but it was no time for platitudes. We went on until we had to pause for breath. Before us, the tunnel seemed to grow darker.

"I've never admitted it until now," Elaine said in a shaky voice, "but I have claustrophobia. Do we want to go any farther?"

I took her hand. "It's hard for someone who doesn't have claustrophobia to offer any advice. Don't think about it. Does that help?"

"Not in the least," she replied with disdain.

"Tell me, how do you cope with the subway in New York?" I asked.

"I take taxis," she said acidly.

Served me right for asking. Still, her typically Manhattan response had momentarily taken her mind off her phobia and perhaps helped stiffen her resolve. She glanced at Mallory. "Want to go on?"

"Yes," Mallory said, and set off along the icy floor of the tunnel. Carver looked at me helplessly. "Nobody asks me," he grumbled, and on we went.

Within fifty yards or so, the tunnel swung into a left turn. We all gasped as we came out into a domelike chamber that could have housed a basketball court. From one side, a stream of water, black in the dim light, poured out of the wall and emptied into a large pool. Beyond the pool was a flat area from which rose a black metal tube. Clamps held it to the ice wall, and the tube soared up into an open space and out of sight.

"That must be the elevator," Carver said.

Two figures were distinguishable at the base of the tube, trying to force open the door. They seemed to be having trouble, and their attention was fully engaged until one of them, now discernable as Leighton Vance, saw us and pointed. Beside him, Caroline temporarily gave up struggling with the door and reached into her handbag.

A shot rang out. Something clanged against the ceiling above our heads, and shards of ice rained down. The explosion grew in volume as it spread through the dome, rising in echoing rings.

"Don't shoot in here," I yelled. "These ice walls—"

The explosion of the pistol was lost in a louder crack that started above our heads. A rumbling sound began in the lofty roof of the dome and grew, spreading everywhere. Then it in turn was swallowed up by the tremendous thunder of hunks of flaking white ice that came falling from the darkness above. Other pieces followed, and the air was thickening as if in a sudden snowstorm while the domed area became a bedlam of unbearable noise.

"Let's get out of here!" I yelled, but neither Carver nor Elaine needed the counsel. I had a last glimpse of the black tube of the elevator tearing loose from the wall high up and folding down on itself amid a shower of rock and ice and metal clamps.

We raced back into the tunnel, retracing the way we had come, fatigue forgotten.

CHAPTER THIRTY-TWO

So you're going to defend Mallory?" I asked Elaine.

"It won't get to court," she said confidently.

It was the following day.

Rescue teams from the Swiss Alpine Patrol were at work in the Glacier Caverns, but an efficient young PR woman had told us that it would take weeks to dig out the domed chamber where the disaster had centered. The damage had been severe but had spread only to a couple of unused chambers, remaining remarkably self-contained due to ice masses a hundred feet thick.

We sat in the dining room after lunch. Business continued almost as usual in the spa. Most of the guests here for the teaching sessions had gone but many of the other guests remained, and newcomers were checking in on arrival. No one seemed unduly concerned and the bulletin released after a night's work stated that Leighton Vance and Caroline de Witt, both employed at the spa, had been taking a guest, Janet Hargrave, on an unauthorized and potentially hazardous tour of the ice caverns when a tremor of unidentified origin had occurred and torn loose some of the supports of the elevator, unused for some time. All three were presumed to have died, concluded the bulletin. The four of us sitting there had no doubt whatsoever.

We had filled in the gaps of the past week for Carver as he sat placidly sipping coffee. Mallory was pale but self-composed, in fact she seemed to have grown considerably in authority. She had spent the morning supervising the staff and was already carrying out many of the duties of both Leighton and Caroline.

I had waited for one of us to ask Mallory where she had gone after our hurried exit from the caverns. She had insisted we go outside, and she had rejoined us a short time later. When the young PR woman gave her report of the rescue team's initial examination of the chambers, we had waited with stony faces for mention of the finding of Janet's body. There had been no such mention.

We had been interviewed individually and then together. A stern-faced captain in a light gray uniform with discreet red epaulets had reprimanded us for being beyond the entry barriers, but upon seeing the furnished chamber in the ice château, he showed understanding and reserved his criticism for the reckless three who had embarked on an expedition deeper into the glacier.

I was wondering which of Carver or Elaine was going to ask Mallory the question, but it was not necessary. Mallory stirred her coffee and said, "When I left you yesterday—" and we all leaned forward attentively—"I went to get the wheel-barrow. I—well, I used it and put it back."

None of us spoke at first. Then Carver said, "I wonder how long it will take the authorities to recover the—the three bodies."

"A long time I should think," was my contribution.

"They may never recover them," Elaine said.

"You think they disposed of Kathleen's body in there?" I asked.

"I wouldn't be surprised," Elaine said. "I'm also surprised we haven't run into your blond bombshell. You don't suppose she's yet another corpse, do you?"

Carver looked interested at the "blond-bombshell" description.

"Rhoda," I said, keeping an eye on Mallory. For Carver's benefit, I described the incidents in the Seaweed Forest and the mud baths. When I finished, Mallory said quietly, "Leighton had flings with Rhoda too—it was never anything serious but—" She caught herself and her tone became gritty. "She would do anything he told her to do. Why should I make excuses for him?"

"The timing of Rhoda's disappearance from the spa gave me an idea," I said. "I think she flew to Paris using Kathleen's name so as to divert suspicion from the spa when she was found to have disappeared. It may have been the same when Janet disappeared too. Leighton and Caroline would want to do anything to keep the spotlight away from them."

"I hated Rhoda," Mallory said sharply. I was glad to see her toughening up after the experiences she had been through. This was a new Mallory now. "But in fairness," she went on, "she may have realized that she was becoming involved in a nastier business than she had bargained for and didn't know it would lead to murder. You're probably right about her flying to Paris on Leighton's instructions but at that point, self-preservation may have taken over. She may have torn up the return ticket and disappeared rather than take a chance of being charged with murder."

Mallory had already told us how she and Leighton had been running the Bell'Aurora when Caroline had appeared. She had found a spa in Switzerland and raised the capital to purchase and modernize it. Now she was looking for a husband-and-wife cooking team. Mallory had blinked away a tear at the memory—not that it was not a wonderful opportunity, she explained, but she saw at once the attraction between Leighton and Caroline. It was instantaneous and electric, she said. Others must have noticed it, but for a wife it was a certain prediction of disaster.

"I was foolish," said Mallory. "I knew, yet I refused to accept. When Leighton poisoned Edward Lester, his partner, I took the blame for him. I knew he had poisoned him deliberately, but I thought he did it because he loved me and that Caroline was just a passing phase. I had the thought also that taking the blame would bind him closer to me and that he would forget Caroline. I was reluctant to take the job here, but he assured me that Caroline would be just a business colleague from then on. Stupidly, I believed him."

"You said you thought Leighton had poisoned his partner because of you," said Elaine.

"Yes," said Mallory, "but I was wrong. They were continually having disagreements over money, although I was the only one who knew that. Leighton just wanted to take control and get enough money out of the Bell'Aurora to be able to go in with Caroline on the spa."

"Poor Kathleen." Carver shook his head. "She should have stayed with her modest blackmail scheme to get free vacations. She obviously didn't know that evidence would come to light that would declare it to be murder, but Leighton knew it was always possible."

"Why do you suppose Kathleen came on to you like that?" Elaine asked me conversationally.

"I wouldn't put it that way," I objected. Carver looked interested in the answer, and even Mallory turned in my direction. "She must have thought I really was a detective and wanted to find out how much I knew about her blackmail scheme," I suggested.

"Are you sure you're comfortable with this solution?" Carver asked Elaine.

"Of course. It's so neat."

"Yes, but it is concealing the truth, isn't it?" he said.

"You're not worried it might affect your career if it comes out?" I added.

She shook her head. "No. It may not be correct according to the strict letter of the law, but it's certainly justice."

"Elaine," I said, "with that attitude, you're going to be one unique lawyer."

"Speaking of being a lawyer, I'd better get to work as soon as possible and find out what this new evidence is that's come to light," she said. "All I know now is that a witness came forward whose evidence was not admissible when the charge was manslaughter but it is now that the charge is murder. I've sent for the DA's new deposition, and I'll know a lot more when I read that."

"At least you know for sure that Mallory is not guilty," Carver said.

"That helps me personally," Elaine admitted. "But I certainly can't use the evidence that proves it."

I turned to Mallory, who was sitting there quietly. "A lot of things about Leighton have come together now," I said. "I know why he had your staffers make the Austrian dishes. I know why he spent the previous two weeks practicing cooking the pork tenderloins and the soufflé and why he didn't allow anybody to come in to the kitchen. He refused to do a TV show with Helmut too—it should have been obvious to me then. He relied so much on you, didn't he? You were really the chef and he took all the credit."

She nodded resignedly. "I felt sorry for him for too long,"

she said in a small voice, "and I loved him. I couldn't help it, I loved him."

She rose. "I have to go and make sure of the preparations for dinner." She seemed taller somehow and more confident.

We said our farewells and Mallory left.

"I should be going too," Carver said.

"At least you got here in time for the final curtain," I told him. I hadn't let him off the hook altogether.

"I have a tentative arrangement to give some talks in Japan next month," he said. "I don't really want to go. I don't suppose you—"

"No," I said, and I must have said it louder than I intended because the echo rattled a row of glasses on a side table.

"See you back in London," he said as he left.

Elaine and I eyed one another warily, like two boxers each sizing up the other. It was a different kind of clinch we went into though, and when we came out of it, she gave me a whimsical smile. "What's the matter?" I asked. "Is this the kind of situation that the existence of your fictitious fiancé was supposed to prevent?"

"He didn't do a very good job, did he? I may have to get rid of him altogether."

"I don't think you even need him," I told her.

"Maybe I'll be too busy getting started in a practice."

We walked out through the reception area together.

"It's a shame we were not able to do a reprise on our performance in the sauna," Elaine said softly.

"Events moved too fast for us, I suppose."

"I suppose."

I watched her climb into a taxi. I headed back to my chalet to complete packing, as my flight wasn't for a couple of hours yet. I was stopped by a voice calling me. It was Marta, all bright and sparkling.

"You look ready to step right on to the set and face the camera," I told her, and it was true.

She smiled at the compliment, then she turned serious. "Did you hear about the terrible disaster?" she asked.

"Yes," I admitted.

Her beautiful eyes searched my face. "You know something about it, don't you? I can tell. My mother was a clairvoyant, did I ever mention that?"

"I don't believe you did, but yes, I do know something. . . ."

She took my hand and tucked it under her arm. "Let's go for a walk and you can tell me all about it. You probably don't want to take a mud bath again, but some of the other baths here are invigorating. Have you tried . . ."